Darling Remy,

What I am goi... ...ou to hear, but p... ... to you in the f... ...s, I have been see... ...know! I know! He was ... ...but we were so young then. Rem... ...onderful to have someone to confide in again...someone who understands the hotel business as much as William does. It started out with simple companionship, but I can no longer deny that our relationship is changing.

Remy, this is so difficult for me. You were my life, my love, and you will always be with me, in my heart and in the eyes of our beautiful daughters. I am so confused. I thought we would grow old together, and after you died, I was prepared to be alone until the end of my life. But now...

I had to tell you, Remy. Maybe I needed to admit to myself that William is becoming more important to me by the day. Oh, my love, so many problems with the hotel, the last thing I need is this personal turmoil. Where are you to remind me that this, ma doucet, *is the game of life and love?*

Could I be so blessed, Remy, to find love a second time?

Yours,

Anne

Dear Reader,

New Orleans has always had her own special magic—a rich, spicy gumbo of tastes, sounds and sights unlike anywhere else on earth. No hellion hurricane can change what she has been to us and it can't change our love for the place and the valiant people committed to making her rise again.

She's still there, maybe caught a little like Sleeping Beauty, beneath the brambles storm and sorrow have cast over her. But she's not asleep, oh, no, not that saucy wench. She's just catching her breath, but some of her toes are tapping, ready to jump up and dance, to let those good times roll again.

New Orleans is different today, in some ways, but the essence of her remains. I am fortunate enough to know some wonderful people there, folks who are not quitters, who will never give in to defeat. They, and so many others have been bringing Cajun Sleeping Beauty, with her wild raven hair and her layers of beads, her flashing brilliant skirts and dancing bare feet, to life again. Let's all pitch in to help by paying a visit and supporting her economy. Meet you at Café du Monde for beignets, *eh bien?*

I loved being a part of this series to celebrate the wonder of New Orleans. I hope you'll enjoy spending time with Anne and William and seeing that love truly can be lovelier the second time around.

All best wishes,

Jean

JEAN BRASHEAR
Love is Lovelier

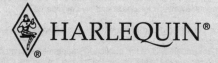

HARLEQUIN®

TORONTO • NEW YORK • LONDON
AMSTERDAM • PARIS • SYDNEY • HAMBURG
STOCKHOLM • ATHENS • TOKYO • MILAN • MADRID
PRAGUE • WARSAW • BUDAPEST • AUCKLAND

If you purchased this book without a cover you should be aware that this book is stolen property. It was reported as "unsold and destroyed" to the publisher, and neither the author nor the publisher has received any payment for this "stripped book."

Recycling programs
for this product may
not exist in your area.

ISBN-13: 978-0-373-18910-6

LOVE IS LOVELIER

Copyright © 2006 by Harlequin Books S.A.

Jean Brashear is acknowledged as the author of this work.

All rights reserved. Except for use in any review, the reproduction or utilization of this work in whole or in part in any form by any electronic, mechanical or other means, now known or hereafter invented, including xerography, photocopying and recording, or in any information storage or retrieval system, is forbidden without the written permission of the publisher, Harlequin Enterprises Limited, 225 Duncan Mill Road, Don Mills, Ontario M3B 3K9, Canada.

This is a work of fiction. Names, characters, places and incidents are either the product of the author's imagination or are used fictitiously, and any resemblance to actual persons, living or dead, business establishments, events or locales is entirely coincidental.

This edition published by arrangement with Harlequin Books S.A.

® and TM are trademarks of the publisher. Trademarks indicated with ® are registered in the United States Patent and Trademark Office, the Canadian Trade Marks Office and in other countries.

www.eHarlequin.com

Printed in U.S.A.

Jean Brashear is a three-time RITA® Award finalist, winner of an *RT Book Reviews* Series Storyteller of the Year award and numerous other awards. Jean Brashear believes that love is the most powerful force in the universe and cherishes each opportunity she's given to share that belief with readers. She loves to hear from readers, either via her Web site, www.jeanbrashear.com, Harlequin's Web site, www.eHarlequin.com, or by mail, P.O. Box 3000 #79, Georgetown, TX 78627-3000.

CHAPTER ONE

ANNE MARCHAND POISED at the edge of the pool in the rose-tinted pearl of the moments before dawn. Artfully-placed lighting cast dancing shadows as a breeze ruffled the fronds of ancient palms in massive bronze planters. Banana tree leaves swished and chattered together like ghosts of ladies long past.

Anne clutched the lapels of the ruby cashmere robe her girls had given her for Christmas and shivered. New Orleans was balmy in February compared with other parts of the country—but forty degrees with any wind blowing, however blocked by the gracious bulwark of her hotel, was still forty degrees.

Cold for her Creole blood.

She thought longingly of her comfortable bed upstairs, the Porthault linens possibly still warm beneath the cream silk duvet from her body's heat. Bit by bit, she was moving her life back to the hotel from the stiff grandeur of her mother's Garden District mansion, against the wishes of her four very overprotective daughters.

This fitness regimen is part of how you prove to them that you are no longer an invalid, she lectured herself.

Drop the robe and get in. They will never stop hovering if you don't keep demonstrating your restored health.

She loved to swim. Was determined to keep her body as toned as sixty-two years on this earth would allow. She had never intended to outlive her beloved Remy by so many years as lay ahead. Had wished, in a part of herself, to follow him after the accident, but for the sake of her already-grieving children.

And for the legacy he and she had put their hearts and souls into, second only to those daughters: Hotel Marchand. Their fifth child was in grave danger, and Anne would not let her go down without a fight.

Anne herself was a survivor.

The mild heart attack had been a wake-up call, alerting her to many surprises. One, that working long hours was not a substitute for proper exercise, however much those hours had kept her going after losing the love of her life.

Another was that her children could be good partners. She would never cease to be grateful that her daughters Renee, Sylvie and Melanie had been able to help her eldest, Charlotte, the hotel's general manager, when their mother was laid low.

Anne had a new and tantalizing vision of how the next years might be spent, but it would have to wait until the hotel was safe. When that was accomplished—and she could only pray that it would be—she would make time for girlhood wishes she'd put aside. She would, as the old saw went, stop and smell the roses.

But for now she had had all the leisure she could stand

regardless that her daughters would like to see her safely tucked in bed or, at most, reading quietly in the corner.

So. *First, off with the robe. Don't think about how cold that water will be.*

She and Remy had built this hotel on the strength of hard work and limitless discipline in all those years when they'd had a dream some people—her mother, especially—had considered a laughingstock.

Celeste Robichaux had had a very different future in mind for her daughter. A suitable marriage, preferably to her dearest friend's son, William Armstrong. Anne assuming her position as a society matron, living her days much as Celeste had, a constant round of teas and bridge and *noblesse oblige*.

But the girl Anne had had visions of the Left Bank, an artist's existence in bohemian Paris, where she would create works of stunning brilliance.

Neither had gotten her wish.

Not from the day that Remy Marchand looked up from a complicated dish he was creating and laid eyes on the intern involved in updating the hotel restaurant where he reigned as chef.

In that moment, two lives changed course. Anne smiled to think of her first sight of the tall man with wavy hair the color of bourbon. Four years after she'd lost him to a drunk driver, smiles far outweighed her tears, though each of them was still smudged by the umbra of her longing for the man she'd intended to love until the day she died.

She shivered again in the breeze and forced herself to put one foot on the first step.

Merde. Anne was not one to swear, but at this instant, she wished the hotel's finances were less strapped so that they could afford to run the pool heater longer hours.

She clamped her jaws together, withdrew that foot and walked around with deliberation to the deep end of the pool. Then did something out of character for a woman with a reputation as one of the most elegant in New Orleans.

She squeezed her nose between thumb and fore-finger—

And jumped, feetfirst, into the chilly water.

WILLIAM ARMSTRONG STOOD in the shadows and grinned.

How like her, that iron will masked so well beneath the delicate exterior. Anne Marchand never flinched at a challenge.

He'd come here, hoping to catch her at breakfast, since she had not spent the night in her mother's house, just around the corner from his, for the last several days.

He missed her joining his morning walks, his frisky young Lab serving as their chaperone. In recent weeks, she had often joined him for coffee in his conservatory afterward, their conversations ranging over a wide array of topics, both surprised by how many interests they had in common. Occasionally she had unbent enough to share some of her worries about the odd series of ca-lamities besetting the Hotel Marchand lately. Her daughters had tried to shield her from the knowledge, but they severely underestimated her skills at piecing together information and forming a whole.

As a fellow hotelier, if on a larger scale, he heard the words she didn't say and did some piecing together of his own. She was gearing herself up to resume the juggling act she'd been performing ever since Remy died and the local economy had suffered after the hammer blow of Hurricane Katrina. Taking up residence at the hotel again was her signal that she had recuperated enough. If her daughters didn't want to listen, she was perfectly capable of charting a new path. Whatever was required to save the Hotel Marchand, she would do, regardless of the cost to herself.

He understood that. Admired that quality in her, as he did so many others—almost as much as he decried it. He felt an increasing desire to step in front of her, to shield her from adversity. Wrap her up and deposit her somewhere safe so that she would never endanger her health again.

But she would never stand for it.

She was beautiful, would be so at any age, but much of what appealed to him in her was far deeper than the physical.

Not that the façade wasn't lovely. Still an exotic Creole beauty in her sixties, Anne Robichaux Marchand had arresting features, her skin tawny, her eyes a bewitching hazel, her bone structure delicate. Unlike many older women whose hairstyles shortened with age, Anne wore her thick, dark mane, richly streaked with silver, long enough to brush past her shoulders. Her hair seemed to match her mood—sometimes caught up in whimsical chopsticks, sometimes simply hanging straight, at other moments clasped in filigreed combs. Her sense of style was unique, and the increasing color in it reflected, he liked to believe, a woman nearly emerged from her mourning.

A widower himself for eight years now, he was not unfamiliar with the process. His thirty-six years with Isabel had been good ones. His wealth and Garden District home put him high on the eligible bachelor list for the city's socialites, but none of them had held his attention for long.

But his Anne—for he was beginning to think of her that way, regardless that she had not yet made peace with the bond growing between them—was a gorgeous, perplexing woman whose layers he found fascinating to peel.

Dreamy, artistic schoolgirl. Driven, competent businesswoman. Warm, nurturing mother and grandmother.

And a widow attracted, despite herself, to her beloved husband's archrival.

Unless, of course, she found out what he'd done.

BEYOND THE SPILL of lights, another set of eyes watched them both.

And plotted destruction.

CHAPTER TWO

ANNE FINISHED HER FIFTY LAPS, her muscles now warm enough that she contemplated simply remaining in the water until the sun was overhead. Getting out would be as painful as going in had been.

But the light was changing from whitewashed rose to an increasingly crisp blue, and she had plans for the day. Still, at this instant, she wished that Zack, the pool attendant, was on duty. He would meet her with a towel and limit the number of seconds she'd experience as a human Popsicle.

Ah, well. She swam for the shallow end, where she'd left her robe, then stood to climb the stairs—

Her robe, brilliant ruby, was held suspended at the pool's edge.

"Zack, you're my hero." She looked up, smile at the ready.

The face that greeted her was not crowned with messy brown hair. Instead, she encountered blue eyes and a thick mane of silver.

"William." She resisted the urge to sink back into the water. A swimsuit wasn't the same as being naked, but it might as well be. And her lines, however hard she worked to keep them trim, were softer now. Rounder.

Would she ever be ready for any man but Remy to see her without the comfort of artifice?

"You are either the bravest or most insane person in New Orleans this morning." Even white teeth smiled from a face that was attractively weathered and increasingly compelling to her.

But still…

"Whatever I am, I thought I was alone."

"You're going to freeze. Get up here and let me warm you." Something must have shown in her face because he laughed. "With the robe, Anne."

"Surely you were married for enough years to know that no woman past thirty wants to be seen in her swimsuit. What are you doing here at this hour?"

"You're visible whether you're in the water turning blue, or up here where I can spirit you inside."

She hesitated, though he was right: she was chilled to the bone.

"I missed you," he said. "And our morning talks before the day gets harried."

When she still didn't respond, he began to fold the robe. "But I see that my impulse was in error." He turned to set it back on the chair.

"Wait." She was being unfair. And she missed their mornings, too, though she couldn't quite recall when they'd slid into them, only that it had been…easy. Too easy, perhaps, considering his and Remy's past.

Oh, Remy…

But William had faced her again, his expression void of all teasing now. A man of great dignity and power. One whose companionship had become increasingly important to her. If only she didn't somehow feel… disloyal to Remy for liking William so much.

Was it always this way for a widow who had loved one man to distraction?

"You loved Isabel, right? Really loved her?"

He seemed startled at first. "Of course I did." Then his eyes warmed as he comprehended her dilemma. "It's not a sin to live again."

She wasn't sure she liked how well he saw into her. Nonetheless, she rose from the water.

His gaze shifted for only a second. Widened.

What— Oh, no—she resisted the urge to glance down. The cold. Her nipples must be— Quickly, she spun around. Barely kept from crossing her arms over—

"Anne," he said fondly, indulgently, taking up her robe again and holding it open. "For a native of New Orleans, you are such a little Puritan. Pretend I'm blind and get over here before that pretty behind of yours freezes right off."

She did as he said, though she had never been a woman to follow orders, unless they intrinsically made sense. She slipped her arms into her robe, still trying to process the *pretty behind* remark he'd tossed off so casually, as if it were true. Instead of letting go, he enfolded her into the soft fabric. Held her for a moment in which she was torn between the struggle to remain apart…and the urge to sink against him.

She chose distance.

William exhaled, then turned her and tenderly closed the lapels snug beneath her chin. Tied her belt tightly, then paused, glancing between her eyes and her lips.

He'd kissed her before, of course, but only the social buss on the cheek so prevalent in their circles or a brief brush of one mouth across the other at the end of an evening. She hadn't been ready for more, though she was certain he was. Gentleman to the core, he hadn't pressed.

But this time…

"William," she began. But she didn't know how to finish. What she wanted.

He bent toward her, his eyes trapping hers.

Just do it. Don't let me think too much.

As if he heard her, he smiled briefly. "Don't be a coward," he murmured, only microns away. "You're too brave for that. Meet me halfway."

She froze. Sudden moisture pricked at her eyes. Once she'd been so free, so uninhibited.

A lingering splinter of grief pierced her. She'd never been with any man but Remy. Never expected to want to be.

But William was right. She'd always refused to yield to cowardice. Faced whatever life had handed her.

Until now.

Until *him,* a man who was starting to matter too much.

"Oh, bother," she said, irritated by herself.

And met him halfway, just as he began to laugh.

Laughter turned on a dime, however. Became more.

More, that was all she could think as his mouth, only

his mouth, sparked sensations she'd thought dead in her. Teased her, taunted. Beckoned her to the fire when she hadn't realized she was shivering in a dark and lonely place.

And she wanted it. Beyond thinking, she merely responded. Slid her arms around his neck. Rose to her toes to bridge some of the gap between their heights.

The man who'd built an empire didn't let the opportunity escape. In seconds, she was wrapped in strong arms, pulled close. Closer.

Oh, how dizzying and wonderful it was to be touched by a man again. Made to feel juicy and ripe.

William Armstrong was one very gifted kisser, if different from—

Oh, Remy…

The man she was used to. Who knew everything she liked, every inch of her body.

She tensed, and William soon followed. Ended the kiss and stepped back. Studied her sadly. "Someday," he said, lifting her hand to his mouth, "you'll think of me without feeling guilty." His eyes were a little hard.

"William, I'm sorry—"

He stopped her words with one finger on her lips. "Shh. I understand." He pressed one more kiss to her hand, then tucked it into his. "Now I'm ready for breakfast, and I have it on good authority that this establishment serves nearly as good a meal as The Regency." He grinned as he invoked the name of the New Orleans flagship of his hotel chain, and the awkwardness eased. "How long will it take you to change?"

If the decision were left up to her, she would have

retreated to her rooms and put space between them. Time to think.

William, however, was battle-tested, once a young maverick who'd dueled with captains of industry, and won. Now he was one of them. He'd grant her space… but not too much.

And she really had missed him. "Give me ten minutes," she answered.

He chuckled. "You forget—I've been married and raised a daughter. I'll start on the paper and coffee and count myself lucky if you're down in thirty."

"Then you'll be surprised," she retorted.

"My dear Anne, it would not be the first time. I've come to count on you for a great deal of spice in my life." Once again, his gaze held warmth and promise, as if her faux pas had never occurred.

Or as if he truly understood.

Maybe he could. Perhaps her love for Remy wasn't the only one in the world. William had lost his mate, too.

Lifted by hope, she winked at him. "Just you wait. I'm not through startling you yet." With that, she crossed the courtyard quickly, headed for the stairs that led to the family quarters above the bar.

At the top of them, she paused. Glanced back.

He stood there, tall and strong.

Still watching her.

HE'D ALMOST HAD HER.

For long seconds, she'd been his at last. The girl he'd known, the one his mother and hers had wanted him to marry.

He might have had a chance, if she'd never met Remy.

But he hadn't been ready back then, and neither had she. Determined not to knuckle under to her overbearing mother, Celeste, Anne had been a willow, bending rather than breaking. Buying time, rebelling in her own quiet manner.

He'd had his own plans, not yet of a mind to settle down. Then the firm his father had chosen to update The Regency's interior had hired her as an intern. She'd encountered The Regency's young genius chef, Remy Marchand, William's rival for his father's favor. Bennett Armstrong had been a firm believer that competition sharpened the killer instinct, that both William and Remy would be honed to a gleaming edge by the heat of their fight for dominance in the hotel.

Remy had won one battle, lost another. From the day Anne had set eyes on Remy and he on her, there had been no one else for either.

But when Remy had abandoned Bennett's designs for a chain of restaurants featuring Remy's cuisine, in favor of owning his own hotel and restaurant, William had captured his father's clear favor. Bennett had pushed William to beat Remy at his own game, to use The Regency's leverage to harm the infant Hotel Marchand, but William had chosen his own path. He walked away from his father's hotel and created his own empire. Married a lovely woman and had been blessed with a daughter, Judith, who now worked with him.

Only after his father's death had William returned to New Orleans and added The Regency to his chain. Over the next twenty years, he and Isabel had lived a good and happy life until he'd been widowed eight years ago. Off and on, his and Anne's lives would touch, if distantly. He would float offers to purchase the Hotel Marchand, but Remy—and Anne, he was forced to admit—always refused them. Their social circles would cross now and again, and it was impossible to be in New Orleans and not know the names of Remy and Anne Marchand—or William and Isabel Armstrong, for that matter. His nephew Jackson was once involved with their daughter Charlotte, back in high school.

But mostly, their lives were separate. William traveled a lot, and Anne and Remy were absorbed in their large family and their business. He'd long ago written off a boy's interest in a lively, magnetic girl with hazel eyes and long dark hair. Now he was much sought-after by New Orleans hostesses and had learned to be careful of the many socialites who wouldn't mind snaring him and moving into the Garden District home that was much too large for him but which he couldn't quite decide to leave.

Then, four years ago, Anne had become a widow.

He hadn't rejoiced as he once might have thought. Her devastation was obvious to all. For a time, he'd considered making an offer for the hotel, but only too soon, he and all of New Orleans had watched in admiration as she valiantly battled to keep the hotel afloat in a struggling economy to which even his own hotel had not been immune. The difference was that he had other resources to bring to bear.

Anne had not. She'd taken out a second mortgage, choosing that over owing her mother money, he supposed. Celeste could well have afforded it, he was certain.

But Anne not only had grit; she had pride. Perhaps too much of it.

She had buckled down, worked harder, if possible, with her eldest daughter Charlotte at her side. Slowly, they'd begun to turn the corner—

Then, last fall, her heart had rebelled. A heart attack—mild, thank God—had felled her. She'd been hospitalized, her daughters had gathered round to take up the slack. She'd acceded to their wishes and moved into Celeste's Garden District mansion just around the corner from his.

And William had decided to act. Many years had passed since their teenage flirtation; more than a few hard feelings had erupted between him and her husband. There might be no future for them or any common ground they could inhabit.

But he had vowed to find out.

"Hah!"

He blinked, and there she stood. "Thank you, Robert," she said to the man settling her in her chair. "William, I'd like you to meet the finest executive chef in New Orleans, Robert LeSoeur. Robert, this is William Armstrong, who mistakenly believes his chef at The Regency is better."

"We'll just have to prove him wrong, then, won't we?" The younger man extended his hand. "A pleasure, Mr. Armstrong."

"I'll have to admit I'm impressed already. My chef doesn't cook at breakfast." William rose and completed the handshake.

"As executive chef, I rarely get the chance to cook these days, but I still like to pitch in every once in a while. Besides, your chef isn't planning to marry the boss's daughter." Robert winked at Anne.

Anne laughed. "Your position was secure long before Melanie arrived. My guess is that you and Charlotte have an early meeting."

He looked only a little startled. "Your daughters would do well not to forget just how much you manage to pick up even when they're determined to shield you."

"My daughters," she said tartly, "would do well to remember who taught them this business."

"Only a fool would wade into the midst of Marchand women and their intrigues." Robert laughed. He bent to kiss her cheek. "Nice to meet you," he said to William, his eyes clearly curious about the two of them.

"You'll see me around more often," William promised.

The younger man's eyebrows rose nearly to his hairline.

Anne merely arched one of her own as she waved. "Have a good day, Robert."

As Robert hustled away, William could only imagine how this would add fuel to the fire of Charlotte's skepticism and Melanie's resistance to any man replacing their beloved father.

Too bad. His own daughter was even less welcoming of the notion, but this was between him and Anne.

Who glanced pointedly at her watch. "It's now fifteen minutes, and we spoke with Robert for at least five of them."

"Two," he said, merely for the sake of argument.

"Five," she insisted.

"You drive a hard bargain, madame."

"When one comes up against a master negotiator, one must persevere," she rejoined.

"I haven't won nearly all I intend to, Anne." He kept his gaze locked on hers.

"I'll commit to breakfast," she challenged. "Then we'll see where things go."

He thought of the way she'd looked in the water, the feel of her in his arms. One of the chief tenets of successful negotiations was patience. He'd had to demonstrate it by bucket loads thus far.

He could do more, even if it killed him.

Anne Marchand was a lot of trouble.

But the challenge energized him. "I'll call your breakfast and raise you dinner this evening." He paused. "With coffee after. At my house."

Her generous mouth curved and her eyes twinkled. "I'll see your dinner. We'll flip for coffee after."

"Done." He laughed and saluted her with his cup.

He kept a lucky coin in his pocket for just such an occasion, one he'd carried since college.

Lucky because both sides were heads.

CHAPTER THREE

"GOOD SAVE, LUC," Charlotte Marchand said to the hotel's concierge as he grabbed for the handle of the conference room door. The phone in his pocket had been vibrating with more frequency as the staff meeting wore on.

Luc Carter had a feeling who it was and didn't want to answer.

A dangerous proposition. The two men who had put him in place here were turning up the level of violence as the clock ticked down to their Mardi Gras deadline.

Charlotte was staring at him, and he realized he'd allowed too long a time lag. "Just doing my job," he answered the woman he increasingly admired, to his chagrin.

His cousin. His late father and her mother were siblings who'd been estranged since before Luc's birth. Luc's own mother, a cocktail waitress, one of Pierre Robichaux's many fleeting fancies. He'd even married her under a false name, Poiret.

Pierre had vanished for good when Luc was six, only reappearing when he was dying. All he'd left Luc was a legacy of bitterness and a taste for revenge.

One that was waning as he grew to know the Marchand women.

But it was too late for that to matter. He was in deep water and swimming hard to keep from drowning.

"Of course it's your job, but that doesn't negate the fact that you pour yourself into the hotel at a time when we really need you." Charlotte skirted the table and approached him. He wasn't tall at five-ten, but the top of her head barely reached his jaw. Those who looked at her and saw only a dainty brunette made the mistake at their peril. Charlotte was as Type A as they came, a restless woman whose life was dedicated to saving her family's legacy.

The one he'd already done much to endanger.

Including stunts like erasing all evidence of the room block for last week's wedding of two very important and politically-connected New Orleans families.

"I'll get to the bottom of this snafu if it's the last thing I do," she told him. "The hurricane badly strained our financial resources. We can't afford this negative publicity. Theft and vandalism during the power outage, lost bookings, the presence of high-profile guests being leaked to the media—it's beginning to feel like a campaign, not just a run of bad luck. If only I could find the common thread…."

The Corbin brothers had promised Luc an ownership position in exchange for assuring that the Hotel Marchand would fall into their hands like ripe fruit before Mardi Gras. Given that his father's relatives had turned their backs on him years ago, that Luc and his mother had struggled to get by when they were owed a portion of the Robichaux wealth—

Once the plan had seemed tailor-made for him to exact a pound of flesh from those who'd been so callous. Who'd let his father die in disgrace and penury. Who wouldn't have cared, even if they'd known Luc existed.

There was only one problem. His grandmother, Celeste Robichaux, was exactly the woman his father had described to him—unyielding and unforgiving. Heartless. A woman who valued family reputation more than the ties of blood.

But his aunt Anne and her daughters were polar opposites of his grandmother. He liked them more all the time. Longed to reveal his identity and join the fold.

The Corbin brothers, however, had a different agenda.

And held the noose of his past behavior, slowly tightening it around his neck.

Just then, the phone vibrated again.

"Everything will work out," he promised Charlotte as he took a hasty departure.

If only he could figure out how to make that happy ending happen with two predators on the hunt.

"WHAT A LOVELY little girl," Anne said to the guest proudly displaying the next in a seemingly never-ending packet of photos of her grandchildren. "You must be so proud."

"Oh, absolutely. If only they weren't so far—" The woman's eyes swam. "Do you have grandchildren?"

"A three-year-old girl." Anne smiled at the thought

of her darling Daisy Rose. "But I suspect she'll have a cousin this time next year."

"She lives here?"

"*Oui.* I'm so sorry yours live so far from you. I can't imagine not being able to see her on a whim." She patted the woman's hand. "Perhaps you and your husband could use the Hotel Marchand for a family reunion. My husband and I raised our children here." She pointed across the courtyard toward the family quarters. "We understand how important family is and do our best to make every guest, however young or old, feel that this is their second home. Have you seen our stock of riding toys?" She gestured around her. "Many a child has played in this courtyard. And for those times when the adults have other plans, we have a superb roster of highly-trained nannies. I've selected each one with an eye to whether I would trust her with my beloved Daisy Rose."

The woman's eyes grew round. "Oh my. What a wonderful idea! Next year is our fiftieth anniversary. What a splendid celebration that would make!"

Anne ignored the stab of pain at the thought that she and Remy had only been granted thirty-seven years together, and those had flown past as if they'd been ten. She found her smile again. "Perhaps you'd like to chat with Denise Sinclair. She manages all our events bookings and can tell you about next year's calendar."

"I believe I would. Where would I find her?"

Anne spotted Luc at the courtyard doors leading into the reception area. "Luc, may I ask your help?"

The guest's eyes widened at Luc's blond good looks. "He's a heartbreaker, isn't he?"

"The ladies do seem to take to him." Anne smiled. "Mrs. Branson, this is Luc Carter, our concierge. Luc, would you please arrange for Mrs. Branson to meet Denise as soon as possible? She and her family might be interested in having a fiftieth-anniversary celebration at the hotel."

"*Enchanté,* Mrs. Branson." Luc bowed over the woman's hand, and Anne bit her cheek as the guest's eyes seemed poised to roll back in her head. "I would be delighted to take you to Denise. On the way, would you perhaps like to see our honeymoon suite? It seems to me a location well-suited for a couple celebrating fifty years of love."

"Oh, well, my goodness—"

Luc tucked the woman's hand into his elbow. "Please. I would be honored."

Well done, Anne thought. She nodded to Luc.

He winked back at her over the woman's head, then led her away.

"*Mère.*" Charlotte called from behind her. "Good morning."

"Good morning, *doucette.*" Anne accepted her daughter's embrace. "How are you today?"

"Behind already." She indicated Luc and the guest. "Problem?"

"Not a bit. After a conversation about her grandchildren, who live too far away from her, I merely suggested that the Hotel Marchand might be an excellent venue for a family reunion. Turns out that Mr. and Mrs. Branson will have their fiftieth anniversary next year, so Luc is taking her to Denise by way of the honeymoon suite."

"He's really good. I thought we'd never find a decent replacement for Alphonse, but Luc couldn't be more suited if he were a member of the family."

"Sometimes it almost feels as if he is."

"You're sad today. Because of the talk of a fiftieth anniversary?"

Anne shook off her *tristesse*. "I'm just fine."

"You and Papa should have had seventy years. A hundred."

Anne swallowed the lump in her throat. "I would have cherished every second."

"I wish I thought I—" Charlotte broke off in mid-sentence.

Her expression completed it, however. At least for a mother who adored her. "You'll find your one and only, *chère*."

Sorrow chased over her daughter's lovely features. "I don't think so, Mama." Anne had come to associate the use of the Cajun *mama*, rather than the Creole *mère* with the presence of strong emotion in her eldest. "You have three daughters who've each found the love of their life. That beats the odds these days."

Charlotte straightened, squared her shoulders. "And anyway, the next love affair in the Marchand family appears to be taking place in some strange venues, like the pool at dawn or the restaurant for breakfast."

"Robert has a big mouth." Anne was not pleased to

feel the need to squirm. "William and I were merely having a friendly breakfast."

"He knows you're back in your quarters here?" She shook her head slightly. "Of course he would. The queen probably dispatched him to return you to the castle where she can keep an eye on you."

Anne knew she shouldn't encourage her children's private nickname for her mother, Celeste, but they were all adults.

And the name was apt.

"She's not the only one who watches me a little too closely for my taste," Anne said with an arched eyebrow, glad to turn the topic from William.

"If we didn't, you'd be back at work full-time—don't try to deny it."

"I am simply lending a hand. It's not meant to take away from the superb job you're doing as general manager."

The temper that Charlotte seldom let free was simmering now. "Mama, you had a heart attack only four months ago, and it's been a struggle from day one to get you to take it easy."

Anne drew herself up to accentuate the inch in height she had on her eldest. "My doctor has given me a clean bill of health. I'm probably in the best shape I've ever been in my life, and I'll thank you—"

Charlotte burst out laughing.

Anne frowned. "I don't find the subject amusing."

Charlotte grinned wider. "The queen herself couldn't have given me a more elegant go-to-hell look.

You have that down-your-nose, off-with-her-head expression down pat."

Anne's stiff shoulders relaxed a fraction. She placed one hand on her daughter's arm. "Honey, I appreciate that you care—"

"But back off, right?"

Anne smiled. "I wouldn't have said it that way."

"Of course not. You're the most elegant woman in New Orleans. The *Times-Picayune* got that right." The merriment vanished from Charlotte's face. "Mama, I couldn't bear to lose you, too. Please." Her forehead furrowed. "Let William take you somewhere for a few days."

Anne blinked. "You don't approve of William. You must really be worried about me to suggest such a thing."

"It's not that I don't approve, only that—"

Anne stroked Charlotte's arm. "I know. You adored your papa. Sweetheart, William isn't…" She didn't finish the thought. She didn't know what William was to her.

Charlotte took her hand and squeezed. "It's not my business if he's special to you. Unless—" Her voice dropped. "If he hurts you, he'll answer to me."

Anne embraced her daughter. "There's nothing serious between us, so I won't be hurt. And you have plenty else on your mind, anyway."

Charlotte's frame was tight with the tension that seldom left her.

"Has something new happened since the booking mix-up?"

Charlotte rolled her eyes. "How did you find out about that?"

"I have my ways. Answer me."

"Not exactly."

"What does that mean?"

"I received another call from Richard Corbin."

"Did he raise his offer again?"

"No. Instead, he issued an ultimatum. He says that their offer will only be good for another week."

"What? *Cochon*. He has some nerve—"

Charlotte smiled at Anne's muttered oath. "I agree. I repeated that we aren't looking to sell, but—"

"But what?"

"Maybe we can't recover. We might be foolish to keep putting him off. I don't know how much harder any of us can work, and I'm waiting for the next disaster. It's beginning to feel like a campaign against us."

Precisely Anne's thoughts, though she hadn't wanted to voice them. "We'll do fine." She knew she was whistling her way past the graveyard, but she refused to give up. She'd fought too hard, and now her daughters were fighting for her. "We're Marchands. The Hotel Marchand is us, honey. Part of our blood and bone. We won't let what your father built be taken from us."

"Your contribution was just as critical. If only we had that money that Papa…"

Anne refused to think about the inexplicable disappearance of funds right before Remy died. "But we don't," she said firmly. "Remy and I built this place with far fewer resources. Working together, his girls and I will keep his dream alive."

Her valiant daughter nodded and straightened into almost military posture. "Damn right we will."

"Je t'aime," she told her daughter.

"I love you, too, Mama," Charlotte said. "Now I'd better get going before Julie hunts me down." Her assistant had a nose a bird dog would envy.

Anne watched as her daughter walked away, pleased that, for once, Charlotte had voiced a concern to her.

And wondered how much longer the two of them could keep deceiving one another with pep talks when all around them, darkness was encroaching.

"G-MAMA!" a small voice cried out an hour later.

"Thank you, Leo." Anne patted the arm of the hotel's longtime bartender, though the gossip he'd passed along was disturbing. "I'll talk to you later."

"Sure thing, Miss Anne." He turned with her, his face wreathed in grins. "So there's my girl."

"Hi, Mr. Leo." Daisy Rose bounced from one foot to the other. "G-mama's taking me to the zoo!" She looked up at Anne. "Right?"

"Absolutely." Anne bent to pick her up, not as easy a proposition with a nearly-four-year-old as with a toddler, but Daisy Rose was petite, thank heavens—and Anne wasn't ready to give up the pleasure.

"Mama, she's too heavy," Anne's third daughter Sylvie protested. "You'll hurt yourself."

"I will not." Mentally sighing at yet another overprotective child, Anne closed her eyes and indulged in a cuddle.

"I love you, G-mama." As free with her emotions as her mother, Daisy Rose snuggled into Anne's embrace.

"I love you, too, precious." In a rhythm as instinctive as it was familiar, Anne stood there, rocking from side to side as she had done so often with her own babies.

How had her daughters become grown women so quickly?

Daisy Rose peered up at Leo with enormous blue eyes. "Mr. Leo, I'm pretty thirsty."

He laughed, knowing exactly what was coming and having the sense to silently consult Sylvie with raised eyebrows.

"As if it would do any good to say no," Sylvie said with a smile. "You'd just indulge her when I left for the gallery."

"Got me there." He turned to Daisy Rose. "I just might have the makings for my special fruit punch somewhere around here. Want to see?"

"Yes!" Agile as a little monkey, she shinnied down from Anne's arms. "I'll be right back, G-mama. Can you wait for me?"

Anne pressed a kiss to her curly hair, a shade darker red than Sylvie's. "I'll wait, but the elephants might not."

The little girl's eyes rounded. "I'll hurry."

"Only a little drink, Leo," Sylvie called out. She turned to Anne. "I didn't pack any extra panties today. Sorry, Mama."

"Daisy Rose does very well, I think. Better than someone I know," Anne reminded her daughter with a grin.

"Sure, rub it in that I was the slowest to potty-train. Not my fault that Charlotte's an overachiever or that Renee and Melanie caught on faster."

"You always took your sweet time getting to any destination," Anne said as she observed her daughter's unique style of dress. Today it was a long, slim eggplant skirt and blouse with an eye-popping lime green belt and scarf. "But your journeys were generally more colorful than your sisters'."

Her daughters were so distinct from one another. They didn't always see eye to eye—seldom did, in fact. But the bond among them held strong and true. That was, in the end, all that mattered.

"Except with Jefferson," Sylvie said of her fiancé, whom she'd known only a matter of weeks. "My head is still spinning." Her expression sobered. "You don't thing we're moving *too* quickly, do you, Mama?"

Anne studied the face of her free-spirited child, uncharacteristically hesitant. "He isn't what any of us would have predicted for you," she said. Jefferson Lambert was twelve years older and a widower with a teenage daughter. "But when you know, you just… know. It was like that with your father."

"I sure didn't feel that way at first." Sylvie laughed. "I was furious with my sisters for hooking me up with an old fogey lawyer."

"That didn't last the whole evening." Anne teased her.

Sylvie's cheeks turned as red as her hair. Anne was sure her daughters believed they'd shielded her from the knowledge that Jefferson and Sylvie had been intimate their first night together, during the blackout. Why did the younger generation always think that their elders knew less than they did about sex?

She touched Sylvie's arm. "He's the right one, that's all that's important, sweetheart."

Sylvie sighed. "Three days, four hours and—" she consulted the ornate watch pinned to her bodice "—sixteen minutes until he and Emily return from Boston."

"I like Emily," Anne said of Sylvie's prospective stepdaughter. "And Daisy Rose adores her."

"Me, too, though—" Sylvie shook her head. "The mother of a teenager—can you imagine?"

"Serves you right that it's one who also has a navel piercing." But she liked it that Sylvie already termed herself Emily's mother, not stepmother.

Sylvie winced. "Thank goodness she's agreed to let the tongue piercing grow back."

"Teenagers have to test their parents." Anne studied the daughter who'd done more than her share, if less than Anne's youngest, Melanie.

"I guess it's simple justice," Sylvie said. "But I thought I'd have more time before I paid for my sins."

"I'd say you don't deserve it," Anne responded with a tug on her daughter's hair. "But I try not to lie to my loved ones."

They shared an uninhibited laugh and a quick hug. "I love you, Mama. It's so wonderful to hear you laugh again. William wouldn't have anything to do with that, would he?"

Anne glanced away from her daughter's too-seeing eyes. She didn't want another lecture. "I don't know what you're talking about."

"All I'm going to say is—" Sylvie bent near "—you go, girl. He's a hunk. One of those who gets better with age."

Flustered, Anne waved her off. "I don't think of William that way," she protested.

"Mama," Sylvie's tone was serious. "Papa wouldn't want you to be alone. He loved you too much to wish that on you."

Anne had to swallow the lump in her throat. She knew Sylvie was right in some ways but wrong in others. Remy had been fiercely possessive of her, his temper as easily aroused as his passion. More than one man had been set straight when he attempted to flirt with her.

And none of them had been his enemy, the way William had. Remy might not want her to be lonely, but that was a long way from approving of William Armstrong paying attention to her.

Kissing her. Making it clear that he wanted her.

"Oh, honey, I don't know…"

"He's a good man, Mama. His eyes watch you all the time."

Anne pried herself from her daughter's embrace. "I can't talk about it." She fluttered her hands. "You go on to work now. All that's on my mind today is a certain young lady I'm taking to the zoo. I'm a grandmother, and that's enough for me, that and the hotel. I've had my life, and now it's your turn."

"You're wrong," Sylvie said, her eyes sad. "But I

know better than to argue when you get this way. I'll leave it to William to make his case." She found a smile. "I think he's up to the challenge."

"Get on with you." Anne shooed her. "We're simply friends," she said for the second time this morning, even though she was afraid she agreed with Sylvie's assessment. William Armstrong did nothing by halves.

But then, neither did Anne Marchand.

Resolved not to think of him again and to cancel their dinner, she turned in search of a little girl looking forward to a visit to the zoo.

CHAPTER FOUR

WILLIAM PEERED OUT the wall of windows in his office overlooking Canal Street, pondering the latest report from his source at the Hotel Marchand. Given the hotel's straits, he'd felt it prudent to have a neutral set of eyes in place. He was as aware as Anne that her daughters tended to gloss over many of the details of what was happening, attempting to protect her from worry.

He understood the urge; he felt it himself. The more he knew of today's Anne Marchand, the more she appealed to him on a personal level. She was the diametric opposite of his late wife; where Isabel had deferred to him, Anne challenged. Isabel had put her energies into the social scene; Anne had built a business. He'd begun to realize that far from being merely Remy's helpmeet, as many thought, she'd been the driving force behind the hotel's success. Remy, true to his culinary genius, had been absorbed by the restaurant and only marginally interested in the guest quarters.

Both women were fiercely devoted to their offspring, but Isabel had tended to live through their daughter, Judith, while Anne's relationships with her girls had allowed them freedom to spread their wings.

Isabel had made William the center of her world, and he'd enjoyed all the benefits, he saw now. He'd never held her back from the pursuits that interested her, he was certain. Her ambitions were simply more modest than Anne's.

Anne Marchand operated on a grander scale. Understood, in a way Isabel never could have, what he'd faced as he created his empire.

The same way he understood the obstacles confronting her now. In her own way, quieter than his, she was every bit as proud and, he smiled at the thought, just possibly as headstrong.

Far from the takeover of the Hotel Marchand that he'd once envisioned, what he now wanted was to help Anne hold on to what she'd put her life's blood into creating.

He could offer the money required to retire the second mortgage she'd had to take out after Remy's death—but he was certain he could predict her reaction. He would still offer at some point, but he'd hedged his bets in the meantime.

He was positive Anne would do almost anything to avoid selling the hotel to the group that had submitted an offer and was having a hard time taking no for an answer.

But just in case, he'd initiated steps to submit one himself. Not as William Armstrong, no, and not as Regency Corporation. He'd resorted to subterfuge, using a law firm recommended by his own chief counsel to keep his identity secret. He was doing it to help her, but he suspected that if Anne knew, she wouldn't have spoken to him this morning, much less let him kiss her.

And what a kiss that had been. He rubbed the heel of his hand over his heart. He might be sixty-five, but his body sure hadn't responded like it a few hours ago. He felt like a damn stallion scenting a mare.

And wasn't that just a fine way to start out a morning?

"Daddy?"

Grin still in place, he turned to see his daughter in the doorway. "Hi, sweetheart."

"Got a minute?"

"For you, always." He gestured to the leather sofa. "Shall I have Margo bring coffee?"

"No, thanks. I'm way past my limit already."

Though he'd originally given her a job just for something to do after her husband left her, Judith had exceeded his expectations. She worked very hard—too hard sometimes. He settled beside her. "Problem?"

"You tell me." She met his gaze head-on. "I came by your house this morning early. I thought we'd have breakfast, but you were already gone."

She wouldn't want to hear that he'd been restless and gone in search of Anne. "I got a jump on the day. What did you need?"

"We had a—"

"—meeting." As quickly as recollection hit him, he mentally groaned. He'd gotten distracted by Anne. Lingered over breakfast and completely forgotten that he'd agreed to meet with Judith at eight for a reason she hadn't divulged. "I'm sorry, sweetheart. There's no excuse. Guess I'm getting older than I thought." Though he hadn't felt this young in years.

"You'll never be old, Daddy." His own blue eyes looked back at him out of a face framed by Isabel's blond hair, sleek and in tune with Judith's always-chic attire. "Where were you?"

Her expression told him she suspected. Not that it was any of her business.

Anne wasn't the only one with overprotective offspring.

Judith was still fragile after the divorce, shaken by being left for a younger woman who was already pregnant with her husband's child. William didn't want to hurt her, but he wouldn't lie to her, either. "I went to see Anne."

Displeasure tightened her features. "Do you think that's wise?"

"What do you mean?" He searched for patience, though it had been many years since anyone had attempted to question his judgment. She and her mother had been extremely close, but Isabel had been gone eight years. When was enough time to mourn?

He reminded himself that a man might take more than one wife, but a child's heart had only one mother. The loss had hit Judith hard, and he hadn't realized her marriage was also rocky. That she'd been trying unsuccessfully to have a child. She'd needed her mother's gentle hand, and he'd done his best as substitute, but he'd felt all thumbs.

He'd spent too much of her youth building a business; now he was trying to make up for lost time. He'd brought her back to New Orleans from Chicago, given her a job as assistant to the very ambitious Glen Schaefer, a man who clearly wanted to succeed William when William was ready to step down.

Until Anne, William hadn't been ready, had lived for his work—but she was changing a lot of his assumptions these days.

Judith spoke up. "I have a plan, Daddy. I've been analyzing the situation, and Glen is all for it. It's what I wanted to talk to you about. But this…association with that woman could hinder Regency Corporation's best interests."

"What?" His head whipped around. At another time, he might have admired the way she stood there, straight and slim and intent on proving herself worthy of his confidence. He'd begun to see promise in her that might make her, not Glen, his successor, once she was a little more seasoned.

But she was still his daughter, and her remarks came perilously close to questioning not only his personal life, but his devotion to the enterprise he'd spent forty years nurturing.

"Explain."

"All right." Reserve gave way to enthusiasm. "The Hotel Marchand is failing. The physical plant is outdated, and the economics of restoring it are iffy. There is a group from Thailand that has made an offer on it—" Her gaze slid to the side, to test whether that was news to him.

He merely nodded. "Go on."

"The Marchands are dragging their heels, no doubt hoping that Mardi Gras revenues will buy them some breathing room." She paused. "I don't believe they will, and recent problems bear that out. The Hotel Marchand's reputation can't survive much more, and I believe Charlotte knows that, whether or not her mother concedes it." Her mouth tightened. "Charlotte's reputation is one of determination laced with pragmatism. I think there's an approach to be made that can work with her. We give her only slightly more than the offer on the table now, but we pledge to keep the Marchand name in place and her job intact."

He would bet money that Judith had underestimated Charlotte in one very important way: her devotion to her mother. Coupled with, of course, the fact that Anne was the true owner and the only one who could sign the final agreement. She had other daughters employed at the hotel and, in addition, a staff that had been with her for years. Keeping Remy's name on the place would appeal to her, but Judith surely had economies in mind. Still, she was animated in a manner he hadn't seen from her since her return.

And he was curious. "So how do you make this a good deal for Regency Corp.?"

Her eyes sparkled as she realized he wasn't arguing. "We cut down on staffing, first of all, then we gut the restaurant and turn it into more rooms, do the same with the family quarters, and we give the guests dining privileges at The Regency. It's only two blocks away."

No way in hell would Anne see Remy's restaurant shut down. "That restaurant has been a premier dining experience in New Orleans for many years."

"We can blend the menu at The Regency and include

Remy's signature dishes. Guests will lose nothing and gain economies that will please them. Today's traveler cares more about the bottom line, and we can cut room rates and still put that property back in the black."

"And what happens to Anne?" *And me,* he wanted to add.

But he needed to proceed carefully. Judith was his child, and he loved her. Worried about her.

"She's retired, or nearly, after that heart attack. Two of her daughters are likely to leave town with their new husbands, and Melanie and Robert could certainly succeed with their own restaurant. Charlotte will be taken care of." Her eyes were bright in a way he hadn't seen in too long. "Glen thinks it's brilliant. Oh, he'd prefer to slash even more—he actually said that it was a pity building permits in the Quarter are so hard to come by, otherwise we could just raze it and build a bigger hotel on that choice spot. But I understand a woman's pride—" Her expression held a wisp of sorrow. "And I convinced him that we had to take that into consideration."

He was proud of her; with more experience, she could be formidable. She'd done her homework, uncovered information about Anne's daughters even his sources hadn't managed.

But…sweet mother of mercy, he didn't know where to start.

One place, however, would be with a summons to Glen Schaefer.

In the meantime, he couldn't make two competing

offers for the Hotel Marchand, even if there weren't all the complications of explaining the existence of and reasoning behind the one already in motion—and the potential for disaster, should Anne ever hear about the one his daughter proposed.

"Daddy?" Judith's look said he'd been silent too long. "You don't like it because of her, isn't that right? Once you wouldn't have flinched at my proposal. It's a good one, and you know it."

Careful now. He took one step out on the tightrope, determined not to harm either of the women he cared about. "Honey, I understand that you loved your mother. I did, too. I would do nothing to diminish what she and I shared. But I have feelings for Anne Marchand."

She recoiled as if he'd struck her.

She paused, then adopted a milder tone. "Look, Daddy, I know you're lonely…"

His own back went ramrod-straight. "So I'm merely a lonely widower whose judgment must now be considered suspect?"

Something in his voice must have warned her that she was treading on dangerous ground. "I didn't say that."

"Oh, you most certainly did." He moved behind his desk in an effort to calm the temper they shared. "I'll remind you that I am still CEO of this company which, I might add, I built without benefit of your advice and managed to make thrive for all these years."

Her face went white around a tightly-pursed mouth. "I know you're in charge." But there was mutiny in every syllable.

"Whatever I feel or don't feel for Anne Marchand, what I do about it is my decision. Not one bit of it is intended to hurt you or show disrespect to your mother's memory, and I would appreciate it if you would give Anne a chance. As for the Hotel Marchand, how much of your plan is intended to cause me problems with her?"

"Someone's going to wind up with that hotel. It should be us." Her chin jutted in a manner he knew he had seen in a mirror countless times in his life. Regardless of his banked fury, part of him wanted to applaud the return of her spirit.

He had no desire to damage that recovery. He'd intended to clue her in about his offer at some point, should he need to exercise it, but not until absolutely necessary, for the very reason of her anticipated reaction to Anne.

He calmed himself and granted her a nod. "Good for you. I applaud, as well, the thought you put into your proposal."

"But you're going to reject it." She was withering before his eyes.

"I didn't say that. The situation is…complicated."

"By her," she accused. "That woman."

"Be careful, Judith." He mourned the loss of the small girl who thought Daddy could do no wrong.

He tried again. "Honey, what is it that you have against a good woman? Do you think I'm being disloyal to your mother, is that it?" He'd always been faithful to Isabel and mourned her passing. Judith's actions were those of a child, not a grown woman.

"She's after your money, Daddy. Can't you see it?"

"You know nothing about her," he said through a clenched jaw.

"She and her daughters are fighting to hang on, but it's a losing battle."

"I wouldn't count her out. All of New Orleans did after Remy died, but she kept everything going." Through sheer will and guts, he might have added.

"She won't, not this time." She paused for a beat. "Unless you charge to her rescue."

The very image of himself on a white charger, with Anne as the maiden passively awaiting salvation, made him grin.

"How can you laugh about this? New Orleans is full of women who want you for your money, none more than Anne Marchand."

"Enough."

And as if she understood that she'd gone too far, she subsided. He fought his temper back under control. "I choose not to take offense that you obviously see nothing a woman could want in me but my money—"

"Daddy, I didn't mean—"

He held up a hand. "I'll overlook that you've decided I'm too old or feeble or whatever to have sound reasoning."

She opened her mouth but fell silent at a curt shake of his head.

"But what I will not tolerate is your assumption that Anne Marchand is some evil person with nefarious designs on me or—" here he had to smile "—that she would ever, in a million years, consent to anyone usurping her authority or treating her as if she were weak. I assure you she is not, just as she has no designs on my money." He paused. Took a deep breath for patience. Then one more.

"Leave your proposal with me. I'll study it."

"It makes sense. You know it does. As a business-man." Her inference was clear—that he wasn't thinking that way now.

She was right; he couldn't deny it. Once he would have been leading the charge.

But it was Anne's hotel they were talking about.

Anne's heart.

All his daughter's questions were on target, her points apt. She was his child, his only child…and she opposed the woman he wanted in his life.

William was not a man accustomed to feeling pow-erless, yet at this moment he was caught between the daughter he loved and the woman who, each day, occupied more of his attention.

"I'm going to have to ask you to trust me in this matter, Judith. To give me time to consider if there is any compromise that could work." He didn't want to have to remind her that he had the final authority. He'd been trying very hard to help her build a future and regain her self-confidence.

But the balance was too delicate. He didn't like what he was seeing going on at the Hotel Marchand, and he couldn't shake the sense that Anne was in danger. He couldn't risk having her informed that he was behind any offers and seeing her back away from him. He'd never be able to protect her then.

"And I'm also going to ask for your word that you will not be a party to Anne learning of any of this. There are forces at work that you don't understand."

When she looked wounded that he would need to ask for her promise, he didn't explain because he didn't want her mixed up in whatever was going on. "How about you and Anne and I have dinner sometime in the next week or so? That way you can determine for yourself what she's like."

"No, thank you." Judith rose, graceful as always, and stood tall as a young queen, her mask once again complete. "As you said, it's none of my business."

Just as he was about to respond, his assistant buzzed him. "Mr. Armstrong? London on line one."

"Ask them to hold for a minute, please, Margo." He turned back to talk to his daughter.

But she'd already made her way from the room.

William swore softly and vowed to seek her out and somehow make this right.

But for now, he had business to attend.

FOR THE SECOND TIME that day, Anne was nervous.

And once again, William Armstrong was the cause.

Ridiculous. She was no green girl. This wasn't a date. It was only—

She pressed one hand to her stomach.

—dinner. Simply a meal between two old friends.

But she sure didn't feel old in that instant; more like

a giddy girl, actually. And were they friends? She supposed they might have been, once, long ago, had she not been a lowly freshman in a girls' school while he was the dashing football captain, class president and champion debater in his own, and a senior, to boot.

By the time she'd returned from college, he was already ensconced at The Regency, following in his father's footsteps, a man of business making his mark in a city she longed to escape. Their mothers were best friends, conspiring so obviously to link their families that he and she were constantly being forced into proximity. He'd been charming and attractive in an intense way that could make her stomach flutter, but clearly not ready to settle down any more than she was.

And then she'd met Remy, and all bets were off.

Forty years later, her stomach was fluttering again, despite her best intentions.

A knock on her door kicked the sensation into giant flapping wings.

She emerged from the cool mint-and-peach oasis of her bedroom into the living room of the family quarters, smaller than they had been when she and Remy were raising the children. Once the girls were all grown, they'd kept only their bedroom and living room with its small kitchen, returning the two rooms shared by their girls to paying guest suites.

Nonsense, she lectured herself as she crossed the room to the door.

She turned the knob. As the opening widened, William perused her from head to toe.

And whistled.

"Stop that." But she couldn't help responding to his wicked grin with one of her own. "*Mon dieu*—I'm a grandmother."

He arched one dark eyebrow. "Do you feel like one?"

"After a day at the zoo, frankly, yes," she responded tartly.

He leaned in and captured a quick, heated kiss, but backed off before she could protest. "You smell wonderful," he murmured.

His nearness was going to her head. Scrambling her brains in a manner she no longer knew how to handle. "I'm starving."

In a glance, he communicated his comprehension of her dodge—and his amusement that she felt the need for it. "Then, by all means," he said, "Let's restore your strength." He paused. "Unless, of course, you'd prefer to order in." Challenge danced in his tone.

He'd been a bachelor out on the town for several years. She'd had only one lover. The playing field was uneven.

But she refused to concede the advantage. She'd always been a quick learner. "I don't think you want any more tongues wagging around here than are already."

"I'm not the one who is uncomfortable about being seen together."

She couldn't find a proper response.

He rescued her, tucking her hand into his elbow and turning them both toward the door. "So tell me how the delightful Daisy Rose is doing, G-mama." His grin was quick and sinful and made it perfectly clear that her attempts to hide behind her status as grandmother were transparent…and doomed.

"She asked after Bo. She wondered if she might play with him and 'Mr. Will' again soon." Sometimes when Anne and Celeste were babysitting, Daisy Rose had joined Anne and William on their walks.

A quick slash of white teeth. "Mr. Will and Bo would be honored," he answered. "Perhaps I'll call her myself and invite her to visit—" a waggle of dark eyebrows "—with the suggestion that she ask her G-mama to drive her."

A dangerous man, William Armstrong. Anne experienced the headiness of being pursued and, despite all the worries that surrounded her, couldn't help but think that she hadn't felt so…female…in a very long time.

"You are ruthless," she said, but couldn't suppress her smile or the little lift inside her. "Now stop flirting with me and buy me dinner."

"Dinner you may have." He captured her free hand and brought it to his lips. "The other…not a chance."

Anne held her breath in anticipation as his mouth hovered over her skin.

Warm breath whispered against her flesh, and she shivered.

He came no closer.

But his smile said he'd noticed.

He'd been around for months with increasing frequency, but suddenly, everything seemed to be moving too fast. If she weren't careful, she could be swept off her feet by this handsome, charismatic man only too easily.

But she couldn't falter now, not when her children's legacy seemed to be more precarious by the day.

OUT ON THE STREET, a man withdrew into the shadows, observing the couple who approached the gleaming black Jaguar. After the woman was seated, her escort shut the door and rounded the hood, a smile playing over his features. He settled into the driver's seat, and the car started with a predator's throaty roar.

The observer flipped open his phone and punched two keys. "He's with her again," he said to the party listening. "Want me to follow?"

"Not tonight," was the answer. "Stay where you are for now. Let me know when he brings her home."

"If he does. They looked pretty cozy to me." He chuckled at his own joke.

"Hmmph." A long drag on a cigarette. "I don't like this. I don't have anyone to relieve you tonight."

"They're old. Chances are, they'll only have dinner, then call it a night. Though she's pretty great-looking for an old lady."

Another pause. "I'm calling the boss. I don't like this," he repeated and hung up with a click.

The observer closed his phone and settled in to watch for girls lifting their shirts, practicing for the Mardi Gras parades just around the corner.

"WHERE DID YOU find this place?" Anne asked as she shucked the spicy shrimp. "The food is amazing."

"It's not exactly your kind of environment."

Her eyebrows rose. "Which would be—?"

"White linens, candlelight. Fresh flowers."

She glanced around at the modest shotgun cottage,

located on a street in a part of town she'd never visited. Its walls were simply decorated with old Mardi Gras posters, and the metal tables were covered with plastic. "We have a candle."

"In a dime-store pot."

"Yet you brought me here."

"I thought you needed messing up."

She was certain her brows neared her hairline now. "Funny, I only thought I needed more napkins." An errant impulse prompted her next remark before she could censor it. "Of course, I could just lick my fingers."

His eyes darkened. His nostrils flared. "Then we wouldn't have to flip a coin, after all. We'll be headed straight to my house."

"Oh?" She didn't look away, though she felt a little like she was baiting a wild animal.

He opened his mouth to respond, but she didn't give him the opening. "What about that corn on the cob you promised me?" *Coward,* she said silently.

With a small sound of impatience, William signaled the lanky teenager who'd served them.

"Anything I can do for you, Mr. Armstrong?"

"Tell Miss Celia she's outdone herself," William said with a wink. "The lady would like the corn on the cob. And leave us with a pile of napkins, please."

"Yes, sir." The young man wheeled to comply.

"Oh, and—"

The boy turned back. "Don't tell me. More hush puppies."

"You take good care of me, Jerome."

"Granny would still be cooking for that nursing home without you—"

Anne realized that William was shaking his head in an effort to forestall him.

The boy frowned. Cut a glance at her.

"Why don't you sit down, Jerome. Tell me more."

His gaze shifted to William. "Well, ma'am, see, I'd better be gettin' back now. Granny might skin me."

His obvious discomfort at being caught between his hero and her forced a laugh from her. "I understand. I'll just work on Mr. Armstrong here, instead."

Relief blossomed on his features. "Yes, ma'am. I'll just be gettin' those napkins for you. And that corn." He made a quick escape.

She wiped her fingers on the remaining napkin. "So you're Granny's angel, William?"

To her surprise, he seemed uncomfortable, something she'd never witnessed in this very urbane man. "There's nothing to tell, really."

"Oh, I suspect there is." She studied him as he focused on something of great interest on the tabletop.

She couldn't help laughing. "You're a fraud, William Armstrong. The big, bad empire builder is a softie underneath all that swashbuckling."

Now he was blushing. And she was delighted with him.

He caught her gaze, and the warmth in his sent an answering ripple through her. "Anne." Layers of meaning, worlds of possibility threaded his tone.

Mon Dieu. She wanted to fan herself. Had a strong urge to run from all that he frothed up inside her when she'd thought what was left to her were years of, at best, peace. Acceptance that she was now only a mother…a grandmother…

Never again a woman in that ripe, delicious, best sense of the word.

Why, oh why, did the man who stirred up her juices have to be Remy's old rival?

She leaped to her feet. "I'm going to get my own corn."

He did a double-take. "What? Jerome will be right back."

Of course he would. But she needed to escape. Order her thoughts, away from William's overwhelming presence.

"I want to meet Miss Celia." Without another second's pause, she made her way toward the kitchen.

WILLIAM WATCHED HER GO, too bemused to sort out what in blazes had just happened. One second, she was teasing him, the next, her hazel eyes had gone dark with what he'd stake his fortune was a passion that was a match for his own…then she'd jumped up and—

A smile she'd very likely term a swashbuckler's slowly curved his lips.

Go meet Miss Celia, indeed.

Anne was running scared.

Which meant he was making progress.

Just then, Jerome emerged from the kitchen with a bowl of corn on the cob, a fistful of napkins and a very flustered expression.

William rose to his feet and waved him closer.

"Mr. Armstrong, I— That lady—" The boy brandished his burden. "The corn will be cold, and—"

William scanned the small dining room. Spotted a mother with two strapping sons. "Leave some of the napkins here, take the corn to them with my compliments and put it on my tab." He stepped around Jerome.

"But what will you do, sir?"

William nodded in the direction Jerome had just left. "Why, I'm going to the kitchen, son." With a clap on the boy's back, he left the befuddled young man behind.

Before he entered, though, he paused in front of the small window in the swinging door. Celia was a good woman, but a tyrant in her kitchen. She had endless patience with her food and her grandson, but little for anyone else. William thought it prudent to scout the territory first and determine if Anne required rescuing from a woman he'd seen freeze a burly deliveryman in place with only a scowl. She most emphatically did not like being interrupted while she was cooking.

He should have known, he thought as he peered inside. Anne had once again wielded her magic. Where he'd expected thunder, she'd apparently not only soothed but delighted. Celia was still assembling dishes and stirring pots in the way only veteran cooks could do, juggling ten things at once—but she was smiling and talking to Anne at the same time.

He pushed open the wood a bit, so he could hear.

"Miz Marchand, no one ever compared me to a French Quarter chef before," Celia was saying.

"Anne, please. I'm telling you that Remy was the best

I ever knew, but you've managed something with your spices on that shrimp that he would be gnashing his teeth over. He'd be begging you to come work with him, I can promise you that."

"Well, ain't that just somethin'?" Celia shook her head. "You want the recipe, that it?"

Anne laughed. "My daughter and her fiancé, who's our chef now, would kill for it, but…no. What you have here is a treasure box of a place, Miss Celia."

"I can't be calling you Anne if you won't call me Celia."

"Celia, then." Anne nodded, and William's estimation of her only increased with the respect she'd accorded a woman who'd likely never even finished high school and was clearly several steps below her own exalted position in the very stratified society of New Orleans.

"At any rate," Anne continued. "I'd want to be the first to know if you ever got tired of running this place, yes indeed, because the Hotel Marchand would be lucky to have you. But I think you love what you're doing, and I only barged in back here because I wanted to pay my respects in person."

"I thank you for that." Celia nodded soberly. "I'm mighty honored. Remy Marchand was a legend in New Orleans food. But Mr. William gave me—"

William pushed inside then. "Celia, my love, is this woman trying to steal you from under my nose?"

"Now, Mr. William, you know I won't never forget—"

"Tonight's shrimp is as magnificent as ever," he interrupted before she could tell all.

Anne shot him a look that said she was onto what he was doing. "William," she said sweetly while her eyes twinkled. "Why don't you just go on back out there while Celia and I finish our little chat." She turned back to Celia. "Exactly what part has William played in this establishment, if you don't mind my asking?"

"Oh, I don't mind at all. Mr. William believed in me when no one else would. I was cookin' at the nursin' home where his great-aunt twice removed stayed, and I was lucky to get that job 'cause I had a little trouble with the law, see, some years back."

"Celia, it's not necessary—"

She silenced him with a look. "Oh, yes, sir, it is. Fact is that I wanted my own place all my life, but I woulda settled for just workin' in someone else's restaurant, long as I respected the quality of the food." She glanced sideways at Anne. "Someplace like Mr. Marchand's woulda been my idea of heaven."

"Thank you. He would have appreciated that compliment from someone of your skill."

"Imagine that. Remy Marchand and Celia Dubois crossin' paths." Celia shook her head. "Anyway, Mr. Armstrong here, he heard Miss Letty goin' on about my food so much that he came to see for himself one day when he visited. Long story short, next thing I know, he's talkin' to me 'bout my own place." Her dark face split in a huge grin. "'Course I thought this is one crazy white boy, but no reason not to hear him out, was there?"

William felt Anne's perusal like a caress. He hadn't

brought her here to learn this about him, but he was resigned now.

"Of course not," Anne murmured, still watching him.

"Anyhow, he tried first to hire me for The Regency, but he has this fancy-face chef from France who didn't want no part of me, I could tell, and I wasn't out to cause trouble for Mr. William when he's givin' me a chance, after all. I asked him to let me do some cookin' for him first, the kind I like to make, as a tryout." The smile she aimed in his direction was bright as summer sun. "The rest, as they say, is history. I didn't see how any bank was ever gonna loan me one thin dime, but turns out that Mr. William was going to be the bank, with extra generous terms." She looked at him, then Anne. "No finer gentleman in New Orleans than this one, I promise you that. He gave my whole family a chance at a future." She laughed. "And now, I think I've just about embarrassed the daylights out of this man, so you two get on back to your table. I'm makin' you a special dessert."

"Oh, Celia, that's not necessary." She brushed one palm over the curve of her hip, just where William would like to place his own hand. "I've eaten so much already."

"Yes, it surely is. I always fix somethin' special for Mr. William, and it would be an honor to serve Remy Marchand's wife."

Anne looked distinctly uncomfortable then. Was it the reminder of Remy or—

He wasn't sure, but suddenly it hit him that perhaps, given the threat to her health, she had dietary restrictions he should have thought about. "Perhaps Anne and I could share a portion, Celia?"

Anne's expression thanked him for the save. "That would be perfect."

He bent past her to press a kiss to Celia's weathered cheek, glistening with sweat. "We'll just get out of your way now. Thank you for yet another amazing meal."

Celia's face glowed with pleasure. "I'd feed you every day and not make a dent in what I owe you. You bring this fine lady back soon, you hear me?"

"I will do my very best." Tendering the hand that had been itching to touch Anne, he kept it light on the small of her back as he ushered her back to their table.

She smiled up at him, and he bent closer to hear her words over the chatter and clink of forks and glasses and plates. "You fraud," she said.

Her face was near enough that he could see the softness of her skin, the fine lines of a life in which he'd had no part. Joys and sorrows, passion and loneliness, exasperation, anger…he wanted to see beneath the masks Anne utilized to keep her thoughts private, her needs buried, her longings at bay.

All the sounds retreated, leaving them inside a shell of silence in which he could feel her breath on him, spiced from the food they'd shared, her eyes wide and open to him as never before. It came to him then that though Anne Marchand was toughened by life and able to withstand its storms and demands, there was within her a fine, gentle creature that had known fear, had learned to guard itself in order to be strong for others.

In this moment, he glimpsed that creature, fragile as a butterfly's wing, fluttering on the currents of an insatiable curiosity about people and a tender regard for their vulnerabilities, understood precisely because she had soft places of her own.

Within William rose a determination to shield her, to do whatever was required to protect the gentle mysteries of Anne Marchand.

And to give her more chances to laugh and be free of her worries. He would offer to safeguard her past the current crises and usher her into a new life, one where he could show her new puzzles to solve, share with her the joy of exploring a wide world for which she had such a thirst. What good was all the money he'd amassed if he couldn't put it in service of the woman he—

"William?" Questions circled in her eyes.

But he was still caught with one foot on the cliff-edge of a startling new vision, and he didn't answer quickly.

Loved.

Could it be that he loved Anne Marchand?

He hadn't thought this day would ever come, yet he couldn't help grinning with the sheer, crazy wonder of it.

"Are you all right?" she asked, and already she was closing in, becoming the person who was strong and alone, who watched over others.

He pressed that hand on her back and brought her nearer. Traced her hairline with a finger that wasn't quite steady. Remembered, just in time, that they were in the center of a restaurant.

"I'm just great," he responded, hearing his voice husky and low.

Her pupils darkened in response to the unspoken message he knew she wasn't ready to hear.

So he rescued her, understanding that he was in for the negotiation of his life.

But she was worth the effort.

And he would win.

He released her, though he wanted to touch much more of her, and pulled out her chair. "So you think I'm a fraud, do you? Mighty tough word to bandy about, Miss Anne."

She visibly relaxed at his light, bantering tone and gifted him with a quick, flirty smile. "But accurate. What else is there that you've been hiding from me?"

He winced, glad for the chance to dodge as he rounded the table. If only he'd known he'd be playing for all the marbles when he'd set his offer on the hotel in motion.

Too late now.

CHAPTER FIVE

LUC'S PHONE CHIRPED later that evening. He frowned at the number that flashed on his screen and merely shoved the phone back into its holster.

"You need to get that?" asked the woman at the hotel bar.

"Nah. They'll leave a message." Not the Corbins, for a change. An international number.

"Persistent girlfriend?" The blonde dug for information, her own interest evident in her gaze. "You must meet a lot of women in your job. Anyone special?"

"Only you, sugar." He grinned and patted his chest. "My poor heart hasn't recovered since you walked in."

She dimpled at the byplay. "Anyone make you register that smile as a dangerous weapon?"

Leo the bartender snorted, and Luc's gaze flickered over, saw him roll his eyes. "Leo, you're tough on a guy's ego."

"Best I can tell," the bartender replied, "your ego isn't hurting for attention."

The blonde laughed. "You must have to beat the women off with a stick."

"Oh, darlin'." Luc assumed mock sadness. "My

tastes run to pleasing women, not hurting them." The phone at his hip started the irritating beep that indicated a message waiting. "You'll have to excuse me. I'm off-duty, but as long as I'm here, I'm never truly off the clock." He nodded to Leo. "Would you please give the lady a drink on my tab?" He turned to go, needing privacy before he listened to news he was sure he wouldn't want to hear.

"Will you come back?" she asked. "We could go somewhere…else, so you wouldn't be bothered."

"Much as that tempts me, it's been a long day." And he was too professional to do more than light flirting with a guest. If he ever figured out a way to stop the freight train barreling toward the Hotel Marchand, he wanted, more than ever, to be able to stay here. He liked this job. This place. The people who were family, even if they didn't know it.

The blonde made a moue of disappointment. Leo, bless him, distracted her with discussion of the drinks he could prepare for her.

Luc headed for a quiet corner and flipped open his phone. Punched in the code for voice mail.

"Luc," the voice said. "This is Ram Singh." A friend with whom he'd worked in Thailand. "I have some news, gossip, really, but you might need to hear it. Please call me."

Luc started dialing.

WHEN THEY LEFT Celia's, a fine, nearly-full moon hung, melon-ripe, in the sky. Its lure was so potent, its mystery so compelling, that Anne felt the call in a way she hadn't since her body had turned from the once-inexorable tide of its rhythms.

How many moons had she ignored since last she'd danced to its tune? How many nights had she been so distracted by the needs of family or business that she'd missed its quiet beauty?

Now the sensation of William's palm was tingling at the small of her back, and tendrils crept along her nerve paths, tempting her. Unsettling her. She was a moth circling in starlight, and he brushed at her wings, rending the layers of protection she'd built up, scattering the flakes like showers of moondust.

She might have resisted the sheer physical allure of him or that effortless charm. In the beginning, she'd suspected that she was merely a conquest, a prize long-delayed in the granting, the trophy he could now wrest from Remy, though the father he needed to impress was long departed.

But Celia had changed all that with one story, and William with his discomfort over Anne hearing it. The warm, giving man beneath the urbane exterior was the pick that shattered the lock on her own heart.

She shivered, as much in anticipation as fear.

"Cold?" he asked, even his deep voice a tangible caress.

Don't make me weak, she wanted to plead. *I have to be rock-solid yet.*

"William," she began. "I know we joked about coffee and—"

"It was no joke for me." He caught her chin. Turned

it up to him. "I want you, Anne." His eyes searched hers. "For many reasons. It's not just sex."

Dear God, was she actually blushing? "William…" She was helpless to explain in any terms but the bald truth. "I'm…done with that now. I'm too old." She forced herself to meet his gaze. "You're normally seen with younger women."

He was silent for so long that she was sure he agreed.

Then he sighed. Chuckled, but the sound was tinged with rue. "I can't decide whether to be flattered that you've paid attention to my social life or insulted that you've just made me sound like someone who needs his ego propped up. And if you're too old for sex, then what am I?"

She started to respond but didn't get a chance.

"I do not for a second buy that you're too decrepit for lovemaking—and don't kid yourself, Anne—" The empire builder stared at her now, the prince who'd abandoned the comfortable castle and scrambled to create his own kingdom from the ground up. "It won't be simple sex between us. You and I will make love."

"You're always so sure of yourself, aren't you? It must be nice." Even she heard the pique in her voice.

The laugh was full-throated. "I had an easier time convincing the banks to gamble on a destitute black sheep's first hotel purchase than I am talking you into bed."

"You're not going to give up, are you?"

"No, ma'am, I surely am not." The buccaneer's white teeth gleamed. "But I did offer to flip for whether we go to your place or mine."

A part of her wished it was just sex they were talking about. Though the very idea of getting naked with a man who didn't see her through the veil of a shared youth terrified her, he was right; she was lying about the desire she felt for him. Every encounter reminded her only too clearly that she had definitely not lost interest in the communion of two bodies. He was more frank about his attraction, that was all.

But the physical realities weren't at the heart of her reluctance; it was the notion that the two of them would connect on other levels. That, as he challenged, there would be more between them.

She could not allow that *more* to distract her, not yet.

"You're going to reduce me to being Stanley Kowalski, bellowing up at your window, aren't you?"

The notion of blueblood William Armstrong, unkempt and sweaty in a wifebeater undershirt, shouting her name from the sidewalk like Marlon Brando, forced a giggle from her.

"There you are," he said softly. "The Anne who wanted to live in Paris."

Her breath caught. "You remember that?"

"I recall a lot of things about you." He traced her jaw with one long finger. "And I want to learn more." He bent and grazed his mouth over hers. "Be with me tonight, Anne. Let me remind you just how young you are."

Oh, how lovely that sounded. To abandon herself to his handling, which she was certain would be adroit and masterful, just as the man was. "I don't know," she murmured, eyes still closed.

He brushed her lips again with exquisite slowness. "Say yes. Let me give you this refuge," he said, as if he'd read her thoughts.

If only… But Charlotte's worried face rose before her. Daisy Rose's trust. All her family, struggling.

She opened her eyes. "I wish—"

"Don't say no," he ordered, and drew in a deep breath as he refused to release her gaze.

"I want to, William, but it's not that simple."

"Tell me. Share with me." Something pained crossed his face. "Trust me."

She studied him, wondering if she dared. He was her competitor, in the strictest sense, yet his wealth and holdings were so much more extensive that she didn't see how her hotel could have any effect on his business. This new ultimatum from the Corbins had disturbed her, but that was a concern she was unwilling to share.

"Coffee, then." He withdrew a coin from his pocket. "I'll settle for coffee." He grinned. "For now."

Trust me. Share with me. Oh, how she wanted someone to confide in, to help her regain perspective.

"Coffee." She nodded.

He tossed the coin twice but didn't ask her to call it. Instead he shook his head. "Can't do it."

"Do what?"

"You're ruining me, you know that, don't you? I was perfectly happy as a raider, plundering ships and kidnapping maidens, until you came along." His eyes sparkled.

She couldn't resist a smile. "So what have I done now?"

He proffered the coin. "Here. My lucky coin."

She frowned. "You want me to toss it?"

"I'm surrendering it as a gesture of trust."

Slowly, she peeled it from his palm. Closed her fingers over it and felt his warmth lingering there. "I could use a lucky coin," she said.

"I know."

She had the sense that he did. That what she would confide might not be such a secret, after all. "Thank you."

He snorted. "Don't thank me yet. Look at the other side."

She turned it over. Her gaze flew to his face, but instead of the devilment she expected, she found him sober.

"You were going to cheat." And he'd asked her to trust him. "You think I'm a coward."

His astonishment was too quick to be feigned, and it mollified her.

"You consider me foolish for not wanting to be alone with you."

"On the contrary—" He waggled his eyebrows. "I think you're very astute."

She could be outraged or disappointed, and either was probably wise.

But a tiger doesn't change his stripes, and a pirate doesn't become a shop clerk. The man inside the Savile Row suit was far more complex than she'd realized. Far more fascinating.

"You could turn it on me," he offered. "Change the wager to whether or not I have to go home alone as a payback."

"I could," she acknowledged. "And probably should." But when had she had more fun or had her assumptions so challenged? Had her predictable life turned on its head?

The woman who'd once been a girl intent on being a bohemian saw the resignation on his face.

And laughed. "Instead, I believe I'll be flattered." Delight danced inside her. "We'll go to your place."

His eyes widened, and he started to speak.

She placed her fingers over his mouth. "For coffee."

His gaze was laser-hot as he waited for her to remove her hand.

When she did, he spoke, and his voice was just this side of husky. "How about wine?"

"Coffee."

"Well, it's a start," he said.

"It is indeed," she agreed.

He handed her into the car, then rounded the hood, his gaze never leaving hers.

The ride was silent, and with every mile, she listened for regret or remorse to creep into her.

But they never did.

"RAM? IT'S LUC."

"How are you?"

In a hell of a mess. "Good. Yourself?"

"Fine also."

"What's this about the Corbins?"

"The authorities in Bangkok—I have it from good source that they are preparing charges of fraud against them."

"No shit." Luc seldom swore, but this news was breathtaking. Terrific. The most encouraging thing he'd heard in weeks. Months.

"They will lose all their holdings here. Face serious time in prison."

Great if they were in Thailand, but they weren't. "What about extradition?"

"They are not in the country?" Ram asked. "Perhaps their property in Lafayette?"

Careful, Luc. No one knows about your deal with them.

"How should I know? I just remember they traveled a lot."

"I have heard that they have perhaps turned their eyes on further expansion in America. I thought I should warn you. Richard and Daniel are not good men, Luc."

Tell me about it. But for Ram, he adopted a breezy tone. "America's a big place, pal. But I appreciate the heads-up. If you hear anything else…"

"I will gladly phone you. I did not care for my stay in their employ."

Then you were smarter than me, my friend. "I hear you. Thanks, and give my best to your family."

"I will. Goodbye, Luc."

"Bye, Ram."

He closed his phone and stared at nothing while his mind raced.

"On second thought, let's go to my place," Anne said abruptly.

They were a block from his house. He glanced

over at her. Even the moonlight didn't account for how pale she was.

He chose the path of discretion. She looked ready to run. "All right. I'd like to pick up something from my house first, though, if you don't mind."

Her eyes were dark holes. If possible, she paled further. "Oh." She stared straight ahead. "I hadn't thought…" She seemed to visibly steady herself. "Thank you," she said softly. "For remembering about…." She shrugged, and if anything, her voice grew quieter. "Precautions."

What she meant took a moment to sink in. William choked back the laughter that was his immediate reaction. The need to protect her, even from her own mistaken assumptions, swamped him. Sweet heaven, how he wanted to hold her. Kiss her. Keep anything from ever worrying her again.

He'd only wanted to grab a bottle of wine he'd been saving for a special occasion, not the condoms she obviously thought he meant.

He pulled into his driveway and stopped. He had to handle this gingerly; he wouldn't embarrass her for the world. "Anne, look at me."

Slowly, but with obvious reluctance, she complied.

He took her hand. "I want you. I've been clear on that."

When he didn't continue, she nodded hesitantly.

"I'm doing my damnedest not to rush you, though I suspect you'd disagree."

A faint curve of her lips.

"I want to spend time with you, whatever that involves. I'm not going to pounce on you."

There was such hope in her eyes that he buried a rueful smile against her fingers.

"You respond to me. I can feel it. Please don't deny it."

Once again, her courage showed in the way she met his gaze. "I won't."

"Good," he said. "That's good." With the unerring sense of human nature that had made him a rich man, he broached a topic that she might find easier to discuss in the darkness. "You haven't been with anyone since Remy?" he asked.

He felt the flinch. "Or…before."

"Or—" Good God. He was going to lose his mind from lust before this was over. He was toast. He swallowed hard. "Before." His voice cracked like a teenager's from sheer, vicious arousal.

It was her turn to smile. "Men like that, don't they? That sense of possession. I'm hardly a virgin, William, even if I have only been with one man. I've borne four children."

"Pity us. We're the weaker sex. I admit it."

At last she laughed, and the tension was dispelled.

"I'm not a virgin, either," he said. "But I will confess to a little more…experience."

"A lot is more like it, I'd bet."

He shrugged one shoulder. "I'm older than you. I didn't marry early."

"But you've been widowed, eight years, is it?"

"Eight, yes."

"You've dated. A lot."

"Probably not as much as you seem to believe. And not many of those extended past dinner or a ball."

She was quiet for a long time. Then she spoke. "Were you faithful to Isabel?"

He caught her gaze and wouldn't release it. This, he understood, was critical. "Yes. Always."

She nodded. "I'm glad."

"I've taken a lot of risks in my business life, Anne, but I'm not a careless man. Even my gambles are calculated."

"So what have you calculated about me?"

"It wouldn't matter." He chuckled. "You blow every blasted assumption out of the water."

This smile was the most genuine yet. "Don't expect me to be sorry."

"Before we leave this topic, I want to ease your mind. One, I wasn't going after condoms." She tried to draw away, but he wouldn't let her. "And two, we don't need them. I've been very careful and I've been tested often."

"I didn't think you were—" She pulled at her fingers again.

"Oh, you absolutely did." He drew her clenched fist open, gently but firmly. "You still don't really trust me." He placed a kiss to her palm. "I will change that if it takes the rest of my life."

"William, it's not that I don't—" She shook her head. "And it's not you, not really. I just have a lot on my mind. A great deal to worry over."

"I know that. I want to help you, Anne. I'm aware that the hotel is in trouble, and you're worried sick." He pulled back and let her hand go, though he didn't want to. "Won't you come inside with me—hands off, swear on my mother's head—and talk it over? If anyone would understand what you're up against, it's me. We've discussed your hotel's situation before." He grinned. "I'm not doing my goal of getting you into bed any favors to admit this, but I truly do enjoy listening to you and talking to you as much as trying to get you naked."

Her soft laughter warmed him. "You've been wonderful to let me natter on in the past, but—"

"You never natter. What's happened now?"

She studied him in silence. Finally, "The prospective buyers have threatened to withdraw their offer. They want an answer."

"You don't want to sell, anyway."

"We may not have any choice."

She looked so small and heartbroken, it was all he could do not to sweep her up in his arms, but that would only complicate things for her.

"Anne, you know I have money. I could help."

Her eyes flashed. "I can't take it."

"Can't…or won't?"

"William, the hotel is Remy's legacy to his girls. You and he—"

Were rivals. "That was a million years ago."

"What did he tell you every time you tried to buy the hotel in the past?"

Her tone had cooled. If he weren't careful, the night would be a total loss, and he instinctively knew he'd have a hell of a time getting her this close and open again.

"He said no, of course. But I'm not talking about buying it now." Trying to, yes, but if he told her that, she'd be gone without waiting to hear why he'd put the pieces in place. He had to think how best to handle things, but regardless, he wasn't letting her go until he figured it out. "Come on." He put his car in gear and drove under the porte cochere, then parked and switched off the engine. Without waiting for her to agree, he emerged and headed for her door. "Rewind the tape, and we'll do the last few sentences over. I wouldn't offer you money if my life depended on it." He found a grin and hoped it passed muster. "Convincing?"

She rose so slowly that he expected her to sprint off at any moment. She wouldn't have to go far to escape him—her mother's house was only a block away.

Not that he wouldn't recapture her before she hit the end of the driveway.

The pirate metaphors were getting out of hand. That made him smile genuinely.

"What on earth could you possibly find funny?" Her eyes glistened in the light spilling from his windows. "I'm here with a man who hated my husband, who's tried to snatch his dream from him more than once in the past, and now you're trying to—"

"I didn't hate Remy," he interrupted.

"Don't you lie to me, William Armstrong. You and he nipped at each other's heels for years."

"It wasn't hate." He clasped her shoulders. "It was envy."

She frowned. "You won. You had your father's empire

all to yourself. I still don't understand why you walked away from it. What did Remy have for you to envy?"

"First of all, I left because I was sick of being manipulated for my father's ends. He had this need to control everything and everyone around him. He had no love in him."

"You were the prince. New Orleans was yours for the taking."

"Some of New Orleans," he corrected, locking his gaze on hers. "Not the part I wanted."

"No," she whispered. "You don't mean—you can't—it was just a foolish notion of our mothers', a pipe dream of two best friends, to have their children marry. You had no more intention of following through than I did."

"You're right," he admitted. "I was too full of my own plans." He drew her closer. "But that doesn't mean that I had no regrets when you took one look at Remy and forgot I existed."

"It's all about claiming rights with you males, isn't it? Marking your turf."

"It was once," he conceded. "And a healthy dose of showing Remy that I could win in my own way, rather than by default when he abandoned all my father's designs for him." He tilted up her chin. "But not now, Anne. Don't even think it. This thing between us has nothing to do with competition. It's more. Much more."

Before she could protest, he swung her around to face the door without letting go. "But at the moment, we'll pretend we're just friends who walk each morning. I'll make coffee or open wine, your choice, and we'll sit in the conservatory, since it's your favorite place, and we'll just…talk."

"Does anyone ever tell you no? Or better, I should ask, do you ever listen when they do?"

He gave her what he hoped was a companionable one-armed hug and winked. "I take the fifth."

Then he led her inside.

Luc lay in bed, unable to sleep. With the Mardi Gras deadline the Corbins had given him approaching in little more than a week, the pressure would only increase. This new threat would mean he'd hear from the Corbin brothers very soon. They were growing increasingly frustrated with him, and he wasn't sure how much longer he could drag his feet.

He needed leverage, and he might have just found it. They weren't in Lafayette, best he could tell, but they were nearby. He'd figured that from bits and pieces he'd picked up in their conversations.

He could drop a dime to the authorities and tip them off to the Corbins' proximity. Somehow he had to figure out what agency would be most interested, and there wasn't much time left to act. Extradition took a long time, too long for the Marchands, but maybe he could cast enough suspicion the Corbins' way to keep them too busy to make more mischief for his family.

His family. He liked the sound of it, even as he recognized that his aunt and cousins would hardly feel warm and mushy about him if they had the slightest idea what he'd done already.

What a hell of a mess he was in.

Oh, Papa, I wanted to avenge you. As things stood now, Luc's quest could, at a minimum, cost him his job, and probably result in jail time of his own.

No permanent damage had been done, however, except to the hotel's reputation. If he could find a way out of this coil and remove the Corbins in the bargain, perhaps he could figure out a means to make the rest up to his aunt. Work for lower wages. Longer hours. He was an excellent concierge, that he knew. He would put his back into it, devote himself to making the Hotel Marchand stronger than ever.

Yeah, right. Like they would actually care about having the family black sheep's son anywhere around. He was nothing to them, however much he wished things were different.

Maybe he should just split. If he weren't around, the Corbins would have to give up on—

Who was he kidding? They'd replace him with someone much worse, someone who had no emotional ties to these women and their struggle.

He had to stay.

And he had to find some answers.

Quick.

CHAPTER SIX

ANNE GAVE UP on sleep at 3:00 a.m. and rose from the bed that had once been a refuge. At the moment, she wished she'd kept the one she and Remy had shared. Replacing it had been one of those futile efforts a widow makes, trying to signal—to herself as much as her ghosts—that she is ready to move on. That she has gotten over losing the man who inhabited it with her.

Blast it, Remy, why did you go off and leave me? But her lips curved faintly as she could almost hear his response. *Now, chère,* he'd drawl with that cocky grin that had first charmed her and never quit, *you're a sensible woman. Surely you see that I would never leave ma doucette, less'n that ole devil Satan catch up with me. For as sure as sin, it's lovin' you more than le bon Dieu that's gonna get me in trouble, but you are worth the price, chère.*

He'd said it a thousand times, that he was damned for loving her more than God, but it was a price he'd gladly pay.

She didn't believe it, though. Remy Marchand was many things, but chief among them, a good man with a huge heart. The God in whom she placed her faith would have seen that and welcomed him to heaven with open arms.

They'd talked about being alone a few times, but mostly she'd dodged a subject she couldn't bear to think about. It still hurt her that he had died with her thousands of miles away, no matter that she'd taken Melanie to Italy at Remy's urging, to help their daughter recover from her divorce. Not being able to say goodbye was a cruelty that was still a ragged tear inside Anne's heart. Her only consolation was that they'd told each other many times a day how much each was loved, and showed it in a thousand other ways.

Remy had forced her to listen, more than once, to something she hadn't wanted to hear. *You are a woman with so much love to give a man. When I am gone, don't stay alone long.* He'd grinned and continued, *of course you will miss me, doucette—how could you not? I am a magnificent specimen.*

She'd laughed and tried to change topics, but on one occasion, he'd insisted that she hear him all the way through. With serious eyes, he'd held her in place. *I'm not sayin' I like the idea of you with another man—and heaven help the ones who might try while I'm still here—but it would hurt my heart, ma belle, for you to be alone when I know what it is to see you happy and safe. Mais yeah, you can take care of yourself, but if some good man comes along who knows how to love you, you take him up on it, écoutes?*

She'd refused to agree, had distracted him with kisses flavored with the tears that erupted whenever the slightest thought of losing him appeared. But when her sorrow had quieted and she'd settled into his strong embrace, he'd whispered to her once more. *I mean it, Annie Belle. You don't have to agree now, but you remember I said it.*

She took up her favorite picture of him, snapped in Tuscany during one of the few vacations they'd taken. *Oh, Remy, why didn't we spend more time playing?* The snapping blue-green eyes, bright with laughter, seemed to answer her. *We were building something, chère, and there was fun in doing it.*

That was Remy. Worked hard, played hard. Sometimes difficult to distinguish the two, as he was never happier than in a steamy kitchen, unless it was surrounded by his girls.

Or making love to her.

There is a man, she told his picture. *A good man who wants to love me, I think. Who tries to take care of me already. He would be wonderful at it, if only I'd let him. But Remy…it's William. How would you feel about that? Would you still mean what you said?*

The face in the photo belonged to a man who had confronted life, head-on, and had done his best to wrest everything possible from it. He'd never flinched from reality, had made her acknowledge it, as well, time and again. *Don't look through the eyes of your fear, ma belle. See what is and deal with it.*

Oh, Remy. Tears gathered in her eyes. *I am afraid. Afraid to love him because it means letting you go.*

She sat there quietly, clutching his picture to her breast, weeping tears she thought she'd exhausted long ago, for the man who'd been her first love, her long love, what she'd believed was her forever love.

But William's face kept popping up, the blue eyes both kind and commanding. The visage that of an older man, something Remy would never be.

See what is and deal with it.

So she held on to Remy's picture for courage and dared to think of another man. And found the end of her tears…the lightness that followed the storm of them.

William's face was a strong one, less angular perhaps than the young man she'd known, but more compelling with the power inherent in someone who has found his place in the world. He was forceful, yes, but not humorless—far from it. Laugh lines fanned out from his eyes and around his mouth. His features were carved by time and battle; he'd fought in an arena she could only imagine and emerged victorious. That he was not ruthless with her, when he was obviously a man who obtained whatever he really wanted, was to his credit.

Then she was forced to smile. Okay, he was a little ruthless, but he was also gentle into the mix. Determined but thoughtful, and had shown more understanding of her dilemma than she had of his.

All right, you…Cajun, she thought with the affectionate epithet she'd thrown at Remy often. *You win. I'll give love another chance.*

She pressed a kiss to his picture, but, instead of replacing it by her bedside where she'd moved it for comfort after his death, she returned it to its original spot on the shelves in the living room.

Then, finally sleepy, she climbed into her bed.

And out again as an idea occurred to her. With a smile, she set the alarm.

She owed William an apology for the detour she'd forced in his plans tonight.

In the morning, she would make a start on finding their way back.

FRESH FROM THE SHOWER, William lifted a cup of his housekeeper's excellent coffee—leaded this time, as opposed to last night's decaf—and took a grateful sip. He hadn't slept well. "You are a goddess, Estelle."

She flicked a dish towel at him. "Oh, go on with you, Mr. William. You're too easy. Sit down, and I'll have your breakfast finished in a jiff. That Bo is ready to walk."

"Always is." He settled in with the morning's paper, but his thoughts were troubled over more than last night's rocky date with Anne, though that was concern enough.

He replayed yesterday's meeting with Glen and didn't like the results any better now. He'd always been an excellent judge of people; the success of his organization was testament to his ability to select the cream of the crop as employees.

Glen was one of those, handpicked to succeed William at some point. He was sharp and savvy and driven, much as William himself had been. Had his argument concerned any other hotel property, William would have agreed with Glen's assessment completely.

But this was Anne's hotel, and every moment spent

in her presence only reinforced what a blow the loss of it would be to her.

Glen's value to Regency Corp., however, lay in his ability to divorce himself completely from emotion and consider only the effect on the company's bottom line. He'd been right to jump on Judith's concept of melding the two properties together. William's daughter was proving herself to be every bit as bright and promising as he ever could have hoped.

But without bringing Anne—and his hopes for their future—into the picture, William could not expect to garner Glen's or Judith's understanding of why he would not allow that cut-rate offer to be made.

His refusal would make a heretofore smooth business relationship rough, and foreclosing the possibility of the takeover stood to rob his daughter of a much-needed success.

All of this, he thought, with an urge to bang his head on the table, for a woman who resisted him at every turn. Who was attracted to him but refused to acknowledge it, much less act on it. And if she actually felt for him a fraction of what he did for her, she was fighting every opportunity to let that bond grow.

If he had a lick of sense, he'd go back to the socialites lying in wait to snatch up the catch he represented.

Too bad he found Anne and her obstacles catnip to a retired raider. He felt twenty years old again and itching to take on all comers.

Damned if he didn't love the juice the challenge of her gave him.

Estelle put his plate in front of him. "Now what's got that cat with canary look on your face?"

He snapped the unread paper closed. "It's a great day, don't you think, Estelle?"

Her gaze narrowed. "I knew I smelled a woman's perfume this morning. You get lucky last night, boss?"

Estelle championed the notion that he needed a permanent woman in his life, and she wasn't afraid to stick her nose right in his business.

"Not really."

"Then why you smilin'?"

He finished chewing a bite of her wickedly good French toast. "Maybe it's just your cooking, ever think of that?"

She snorted as she wiped her hands on her apron. "You been eatin' my cookin' for seven and a half years now, but I haven't seen that particular smile ever before. It's got *woman* written all over it."

"That's for me to know and you to find out." Though he'd learned long ago that secrets from Estelle were few and far between.

She pointed a finger at him. "And don't you think I won't. Now you gonna invite Miss Anne in, or shall I?"

His head jerked up. "Anne? She's here?" He rose.

"Right out on the porch."

He dropped his napkin and rounded the table. "How long has she been there? Why didn't you let her in?"

"'Cause she just this minute walked up the steps."

He was nearly to the dining room door when she called after him. "Miss Anne better be some part of that smile you had, is all I got to say. I like that woman. She's different from those bottle blondes always pantin' after you."

But William wasted no time arguing; instead, he called for Bo.

"Wait—you didn't finish. And Miss Anne might need to eat, too."

She was right on both counts, but he didn't want their first encounter after last night to be in the presence of others.

Bo didn't count; he wouldn't carry tales. William had no idea why Anne would be here this morning.

"Estelle, I apologize for wasting that good food." He faced her as Bo wriggled beside him. "But I need to see Anne alone first."

She waved him off. "I can make more. You go on and bring her back with you, you hear?"

"Yes, ma'am."

"All right, then. Have a good walk. And you mind your manners, Bo. Miss Anne's a lady, through and through."

William returned her wave and opened his front door.

Anne turned at the sound, one hand against the white Doric column as if she needed bracing. There were dark smudges beneath her eyes.

"Are you all right?" He closed the distance between them.

She didn't quite smile as she met his gaze earnestly. "You always think of me first, don't you?" Before he could answer, she went on. "I didn't sleep well. I owe you an apology."

This wasn't how he'd anticipated their next encounter proceeding. "For what?"

"Where shall I start? For crying on your shoulder but refusing to let you help with my business concerns?"

"Changed your mind?"

"No." She did smile then. "But I appreciate the gesture more than you can imagine. It's wonderful just to be able to voice my worries to someone who understands their context, someone who can help me put them in perspective. I've never had that."

"Never?"

She took a deep breath, let it out. "Remy and I were partners in everything, but not equal ones. He had too much on his plate with running the restaurant and being its chef. He had to be both manager and culinary genius. He was superb at both, but—" She shrugged.

"That left you running the hotel. A daunting task on its own."

Her smile was grateful. "We made the big decisions together, but the day-to-day…"

"Can be a real grind."

She seemed surprised.

"You weren't there to see it, but I did that on my first two hotels. It was a few years before I could afford to step back from the day-to-day and assume a strictly oversight position."

"No wonder you understand so much." She glanced away. "But there's another apology I must make, and it's a harder one. About…last night…"

"You don't owe me anything. I pushed, and you weren't ready."

She straightened. Cocked her head. "I led you on, so maybe we're even."

A dull ache settled in. *Led you on.* She might never be ready for more than friendship, and he had to accept that.

"We're still friends, aren't we?" he asked. "We'll leave it at that. Bo's ready for his walk, as you can see." Bo had, by now, wound his leash around both of them. "So, after you, madame." He began to untangle them.

"Wait." She stopped him with one slim hand on his arm. "You're giving up? Just like that?"

What the hell do you want from me, woman? he wanted to roar. "Anne, you've made yourself clear. You enjoy my company, but that's all you'll commit to. That's fine. I'm a realist. I value—"

Whatever he'd thought to say was swallowed up when she stood on tiptoe and kissed him. Hard.

William didn't waste time asking questions. He dropped Bo's leash and grabbed her. Kissed her back.

Whoa. The kiss went on and on, and every last thought but one drained from his head.

He'd go to his grave wanting her. And damned if he was giving up.

He was on the verge of sweeping her into his arms and charging up the stairs to his bedroom when Bo barked.

"Anne Robichaux, what on earth are you doing?"

Her battle-ax mother Celeste stood on the sidewalk, hands on her hips.

William swore in three languages. But he didn't let

her go. "She's kissing me, Celeste." Anne's head was buried against his chest, and he felt her shaking.

"On the street—in view of everyone we know," Celeste complained.

"On my porch, Celeste. Not one car has passed." Not that he cared, but Anne might. Mentally he beseeched the heavens for a lightning strike at that moment.

Then he sighed, knowing that Bo still had to be exercised. "If you'll excuse us, we'll continue with our walk. I'd invite you to accompany us—" *when hell froze over* "—but I know that you don't care for dogs."

"You'll come see me afterward, Anne." No queen was ever more imperious.

He felt Anne tense to turn and respond, but he intervened, still holding her close. "I regret to tell you that Anne has agreed to accompany me to a meeting where her input will be invaluable." He smiled to remove the sting. "But I'm certain she will be talking to you soon. She's a good daughter."

With a slow, satisfied smile Celeste shifted her gaze between Anne and himself. If a black widow spider could produce a smile, it would surely resemble something like Celeste Robichaux's. William was reminded vividly that once this woman and his mother had conspired to accomplish exactly this result: Anne in his arms. In his life.

On that, he and Celeste were in perfect agreement. The fly in the ointment was that Anne had rebelled against her mother's schemes more than once in her life, so Celeste's backing might actually harm his cause.

Celeste nodded at him as if the idea had occurred to her, too. "She's my only child, and I'm grateful for her."

William felt Anne flinch at the falsehood. Celeste had another child, a son whom she'd banished, the brother Anne still longed to find. He squeezed her arm and answered in her stead. "Good morning to you, then, Celeste. We'll just be on our way." *Not to the heaven I'd envisioned a few moments ago, thanks to you*, he resisted saying.

Celeste studied the two of them a second longer. *"Au revoir."* And she was off.

Anne's trembling frame parted from him, and he prepared to soothe her.

Turned out, he couldn't have been more wrong. She burst into gusts of laughter she'd obviously been re- straining. "Caught like a couple of kids on Lovers Lane," she blurted between whoops. "Oh, lordy, what I wouldn't give for a picture of her face. *Anne Robichaux, what on earth are you doing?*" she mimicked.

He had no choice but to join her. Bo whirled in circles and barked, and they both laughed so hard they collapsed on the wicker swing behind them. William couldn't recall the last time he'd felt this good. This lighthearted.

At last, they wound down to small, intermittent chuckles.

The morning silence wove between them, around them, encasing them in a universe where he was su- premely aware of the rise and fall of her breasts, the heat of her body beside his.

The pure rightness of all of it, Anne here, in his home. His life.

She spoke first. "My input will be invaluable?" Her teasing tone brought his head around. She ran her tongue over her teeth. "Exactly where is this meeting?"

The mischief in her gaze lightened his heart almost enough to make up for the exasperation of Bo tugging on his leash. "Would you be scandalized if I said upstairs in the master suite?"

He was ready, so ready to make love to her. To make her his.

"Would you be scandalized if I said the idea has appeal?"

He swore his heart stopped. He had to get this absolutely clear. "You said you led me on last night."

"I didn't mean to, but I was confused."

"Are you confused now?"

An endless pause. "Not so much."

"How much?"

"A little," she admitted. "Should I leave?"

"Not a chance." He grabbed her before she could move. "A little, I can live with." He flashed her a grin and cautioned himself to take things slow. If it killed him.

Which he was sure it would. "Let's walk this dog. Then I'm under orders from Estelle to bring you in and feed you."

"And then what?"

He glanced down at her, liking the feel of her tucked into his side. "Then I work on whittling down *a little* into *no doubts at all.*"

"Careful with that ego, Mr. Armstrong. There are some low branches on our route."

"But you'll comfort me if I come to harm, won't you? Tear your petticoats and bind my wounds?"

She chuckled. "I'll keep Bo from slobbering on you. My petticoats disappeared after my debutante ball."

"Why, Miss Anne, you surrendered your petticoats?" he said in as near a falsetto as he could manage. "I do believe I am scandalized, after all."

Bo tugged, and they followed him.

Laughing once more.

CHAPTER SEVEN

BREAKFAST WITH WILLIAM was a lighthearted—and potentially fattening—affair. How he kept himself in such good shape with delicious food like this always at hand, Anne wasn't sure. She could only manage by taking much less of Estelle's to-die-for French toast than she wanted.

"It tastes like sin, but Estelle is a wizard with substitutions." William indicated the toast with his fork. "You'd be surprised how low the fat and caloric content of that is."

"Ah. Your secret weapon. I'd wondered."

"Wondered what?"

The arched eyebrow made her blush. "Nothing."

"Play fair, Anne."

She stared at her plate. Then forced her gaze upward. "How you stay in such great shape."

A quick, delighted grin. Then a poke at her embarrassment. "So you've been looking me over?"

"Oh, bother." She glanced out the window. "So what if I have?"

The teasing glow heated into more. "So I like it. You thinking about me." He shrugged. "It's only fair, after all. I spend an inordinate amount of time admiring you."

Her gaze shifted. "You do?"

"You've stolen more than a few hours of sleep from me, Anne." He laced their fingers. "This experience is as new to me as it is to you," he said, low and husky. "Most men marry again very soon after they lose a mate. I'd never intended to. Not because I didn't enjoy being married, but just—" He raised their locked hands to his lips. "I'm a very selective man. I've always had a taste for the…special. The unique." His warm mouth brushed her knuckles. "I hadn't found that until you."

She was a little breathless. "I'm not extraordinary."

"Oh, but you are, my darling. You absolutely are. Shall I enumerate the ways?"

She tugged at his hand, face hot. "I don't think so." She was still trying to absorb the *my darling*.

His grin was fond and quick. "Actually, it might do you good. You may poke fun at my ego, but yours has remained remarkably modest when by all rights it shouldn't be. You're a beautiful woman with a privileged background and every reason to expect a pampered life. Instead, not only do you create an exceptional hotel with guests who return year after year precisely because the experience you give them is unique, but you bear four lovely, bright and capable daughters, choosing to rear them yourself with minimal outside help. And you made one man extremely happy in a partnership that few understood but many envied." He was all seriousness now. "Including me."

Her eyes stung. "Thank you for that. Especially for acknowledging Remy. I—William, if we're to make something of this, I need to be able to speak of him without worrying about the impact on you."

He nodded. "The same goes for Isabel. They both existed, Anne. They were important to us. We passed much of our lives with them, and that made us who we are." His lips curved. "I like who you are."

Relief was a cooling wind. "And I like you." She swallowed hard. "Maybe more than like."

His pupils darkened. "I want that *more*. A lot of it." His fingers squeezed hers. "I'm moving as slow as I can manage, but I want credit. It's damn hard. When I see something I want, I've never rested until I had it."

"I'm not a possession."

He shook his head. "That you most certainly are not. You're work, Anne, a lot of it."

"Too much?"

He chuckled. "Not on your life." He eased his hand from hers, tracing one finger over the back of it. "Now, much as I'm ruing my decision to stay active in my business when most men would be retired, I have a meeting I can't miss."

She couldn't resist casting her eyes toward the staircase. "Not the previously-referenced meeting involving me, I assume?"

"As if I didn't already regret the need not to cancel the one downtown." He tapped a fist to his heart. "You're killing me, you evil woman."

"I thought I was unique and special." She rose and placed her napkin on the table.

"That, too." He followed suit.

"Well, I have a date with my mother, it seems."

"Oh, ouch. Maybe I could shuffle my meeting back a little. Be your bodyguard."

"I only wish, but no…I have to do this all by myself."

"I don't believe in others taking punishment for my misdeeds."

"As I recall, I kissed you first."

His gaze lit again. "And I will thank you for that for some time to come." He sobered. "Truly, I would accompany you if you asked."

She smiled and cupped one hand to his jaw. "I believe you. It won't be necessary, I promise. My mother doesn't frighten me."

"I said you were unique. Half of New Orleans is terrified of her. The other half hasn't met her."

Laughter bubbled up, and she was struck by how long it had been since she'd laughed this much in one day. "My mother still thinks you're Prince Charming. I'd lay money on that."

"Don't hold it against me, okay?"

She was delighted that he seemed honestly worried that she would. She rose to her toes and pressed a brief kiss to his cheek. "I won't. Have a great day."

"Wait, wait, wait." He grabbed her around the waist, hauled her to him. "Let's make plans. I know you spend much of the day at the hotel now and my schedule's tight, too, but are you free tonight?"

"Why, Mr. Armstrong, are you asking me for a date?"

"I'd admit to a little worry over using that word. You might say no. You have before."

She peeled away, amazed at how much fun flirting could be. "Try me," she cast over her shoulder.

"Pick you up at seven-thirty."

She glanced back. Enjoyed the sight of him, so tall and strong. "How shall I dress?"

"Is naked an option?"

"William!" She cut a glance toward the kitchen. "Estelle," she hissed.

"Estelle likes you. She thinks you're a lady."

"She won't if you keep this up."

"She believes you're good for me. She won't quarrel with my methods of securing your presence here."

He was so arrogant he took her breath away sometimes.

He was also wonderful. And fun.

And two could play. "She's not a live-in, right?"

Even across the room, she saw his eyes darken at the inference. "No. And she could have a lot of days off, if that's important."

"You'd be sorry. I can't cook."

He began to move toward her, a panther on the prowl. "I have a phone and a wallet. Or an entire hotel kitchen staff at my disposal."

She backed away. "We're getting ahead of ourselves."

His voice was low, his gaze intent. "Then you'd better run, little girl. 'Cause I'm just getting up to speed."

"You don't scare me—" He pounced, and she squealed.

Just before he cut off her breath with a kiss that melted all her wiring, his body plastered against hers, her back to the wall.

After her synapses shot into overload, finally, he

eased away, mere inches between them. "Dress up," he said so casually she would have thought she'd dreamed what had just happened if she couldn't still feel his body's reaction to her.

And hers to him. She let her breath out, long and slow. "Whew."

He laid his forehead against hers. "Yeah."

"Well, then. I guess—" She still couldn't think straight. She slipped her wrists from the big hands that had circled them. "I should—"

He smiled. "Yeah. Me, too."

"May I leave my car where it is?"

"That mouthwatering red Corvette?" He shook his head. "Bait for a car thief, for sure."

She flushed. "It was Remy's. I couldn't bring myself to sell it, so when times got hard, I sold my car instead. I know it's too young—"

"We're as young as we feel. Me, I feel about sixteen at the moment. Sure thing, leave it while you face the executioner. Or if you'd prefer to move it to my drive, I can switch my car before you go."

"No. I won't be long. I hope." She was surprised by how much she didn't want to leave. "You'll tell Estelle goodbye for me? And thanks again for the yummy meal?"

"I will." He reached for her hand. "It's going to be a long day."

She all but danced backward. "No touching. You're too dangerous."

A wide, delighted grin split his face. "I'm not the only one."

She whirled before she gave in to the impulse to stay. They both had responsibilities. She was astonished at how completely he'd taken her mind off the hotel's troubles.

"Anne, wait."

She paused, one hand on the doorknob.

"Thank you," was all he said. "For coming to me this morning. I know it wasn't easy."

She looked back over her shoulder. "I'm working on…all of this. I promise."

He nodded, and she thought he really might understand. "Have a wonderful day." He grinned. "Call me if you need reinforcements with Celeste."

She groaned. "Don't remind me." She smiled back. "Have a lovely day yourself. I'll see you tonight."

"I'll be counting the hours," he said.

She walked down his steps, realizing that she would be, too.

ANNE WALKED the block to her mother's home, still bemused by the morning's events. Nothing Celeste would say could possibly rattle her as thoroughly as her own behavior had.

As William had.

She touched her lips and fought a secret smile. They were tender. Ultrasensitive. Still alive and tingling a bit, however absurd that might sound.

The man could kiss. He had a way with his hands, as well. He was a man who was confident in his skills, secure in who he was and what he'd accomplished.

And he found her extraordinary.

She might be sixty-two and a grandmother, but she was feeling just a bit giddy right now.

Then she opened her mother's front gate, and her euphoria drained away.

"Ridiculous, Anne." She lectured herself all the way up the front walk. She'd learned to handle her mother long ago, at least as well as anyone ever had. Her father had chosen the path of least resistance with his overbearing, opinionated wife, and Anne's brother Pierre had suffered for it. He'd been a handful as a small boy and real trouble when he got older; Celeste had been so determined to force him onto the right path that she'd been extremely harsh on him.

Anne had spent her childhood protecting her adored younger sibling. Being obedient herself had bought them both some cover. She'd been the perfect Creole princess, rising to the ultimate heights as Queen of the Crewe of Rex during Carnival after a brilliant debutante season.

All the while dreaming of Paris and a garret. Of a starving artist's life. Of side trips to Florence, where she would replenish her soul for the stunning works she would paint. She'd been talented, maybe more than a little.

But their father had died when Anne was seventeen. Her younger brother, Pierre, had walked out the door a few years later and had never been seen again. Though her mother was hardly easy, she was alone then. Anne had tried to offer her support, but by this point she had met and married Remy Marchand, walking away from both her mother's plans for her—and her own.

Nothing had mattered but Remy.

The early years had been rough, not only with the endless hours and struggle required to get their hotel on its feet but the chill between herself and her mother. They'd gone months without speaking. No telling how long it might have lasted, if not for Charlotte.

Celeste's inflexibility crumbled like an aging brick wall when her first grandchild came into the picture. She and Anne mended fences. Anne had never enjoyed holding a grudge, though her mother could do so endlessly.

Celeste had installed herself as a fixture in their lives and welcomed each child as she was born. If she ever thought about the son she had cast from her life, Anne couldn't tell it. Celeste was too busy meddling in Anne's family, attempting in her not-always-subtle ways to mold her granddaughters into the path she'd kept Anne on until that fateful meeting with the odious Cajun who'd stolen her daughter's heart. That Celeste and Remy got along at all was more a credit to Remy than Celeste, though she'd made her peace with the man who'd fathered her new hopes for a proper society princess.

Anne had come to her daughters' rescue countless times as their *grand-mère* interfered in their lives. One could not be faint of heart and deal successfully with the Queen.

She would survive this encounter, too, but it wouldn't be fun.

The front door flew open just as she lifted her hand toward the ancient brass knocker, gleaming as always.

"I hear you've been a very bad girl." Renee's blue eyes sparkled with merriment.

"Oh, thank God. Reinforcements." Anne's embrace was perhaps more ardent than usual. Renee and Celeste had only recently come to a *rapprochement* after years of difficulty. She would be a welcome buffer.

"Oh, I don't know, Mom." Her strawberry-blond daughter, slim and taller than Anne, pretended to think. "I should probably get to work immediately to deal with the flood of tabloid reporters. I can just see the headlines now—St. Anne a Fallen Woman? Or no, wait— William the Conqueror Has His Way—"

"Don't start with me." But Anne couldn't hold firm again her child's amusement. Charlotte would be standing beside Celeste, frowning, but Renee, even before her years in Hollywood, had been much less judgmental. "But you might want to leave before the shouting starts."

"Are you kidding? I wouldn't miss this for a shot at the cover of *Condé Nast Traveler*." Renee leaned over as they walked down the long hall toward the execution chamber. "Of course, this escapade is more likely to be on the front page of the *Enquirer*."

"Very funny."

"You don't mind if I set up a conference call on my cell phone, so I can broadcast the pictures to the others?"

Anne's head whipped around, then she had to smile at how much Renee was enjoying this. "Don't get cocky, *doucette*. You know one of us is always in trouble with her. You haven't been in her good graces that long. Things could change."

"I'm not worried. All I have to do is say the word *wedding,* and it's instant favorite grandchild status."

"Only if you and Pete don't elope. And you agree to invite no less than five hundred."

Renee grimaced. "You're a sore loser, Mom."

"Actually—" Anne paused before the parlor doors and patted her daughter's cheek. "I'm feeling pretty lucky this morning."

"Mom!" Her daughter's eyes popped wide, and it was all Anne could do not to laugh. "Why, you hussy." Renee rubbed her hands together. "Okay, I'll be your decoy, but you have to dish details as soon as we escape."

"Oh, *chère.*" Anne hugged her again and held on. "I am so happy to have you here with us. I know you and Pete will have to return to L.A. soon, but—"

Renee tightened her grip. "No, Mama, we don't."

"What are you saying?"

"As a top-notch director, Pete's in demand, yes, and he has to travel a lot, but he understands the importance of family. He knows we all have to pull together right now to make the hotel's future sound, and he says he can just as easily have New Orleans as his home base."

Anne's eyes stung suddenly. "Oh, *bébé.* I wouldn't have asked—"

Renee kissed her cheek. "I know. You don't have to, Mom. We love you, all of us. We admire how you kept going after Papa died. We want to be here for you."

"Then I'm more than lucky today. I'm truly blessed."

"Is that you, Anne?" Celeste's voice came from behind the door.

Anne sighed. Rolled her shoulders like a boxer. "*Oui, Mère.*"

"I've got your back," Renee whispered and squeezed her hand. "And anyway, we can run faster than she can."

They were both trying to stifle their giggles as Anne opened the door.

WILLIAM WAS on his way downtown immediately after Anne left. He'd sent an e-mail last night to Jud Lawson, the attorney who was serving as trustee for his offer on the Hotel Marchand, requesting that the lawyer he'd hired for this one purpose clear time for him as soon as possible today. First thing this morning, there'd been an answer that Jud had pushed all his appointments back and would be available as early as William cared to arrive.

There were benefits to being a powerful man. William was not averse to trading upon them when needed, and now was such a time. The desperation in Anne's voice last night when she'd spoken of the demand Charlotte had received worried him. Anne didn't want to sell; he knew that. But rather than jeopardize the financial welfare of her daughters, she very well might force herself to accept the loss of Remy's dream. Her dream. At base, he was certain that what she and Remy had wanted, as all good parents did, was to give their children as secure a future as possible. Anne had proven willing to take risks for herself, but he doubted that extended to her girls. If the hotel's future seemed doomed, she would cast aside those dreams in favor of cashing out for whatever she could recoup.

She deserved better. If she had another offer in hand, a decent one, with no urgency attached, perhaps she would feel the freedom to hang on for a while, and matters might improve. She and her girls were working hard to steady the hotel's footing, and he would never bet against Anne Marchand.

Especially not when it gave him more time to lend his own influence toward that end. If she wouldn't accept money from him, he could be there to encourage her, yes, and he would. But he also had the ear of suppliers they held in common, and giving them a nudge to offer her more favorable terms or ride with her longer would be easy enough for him to do.

A delicate balance would be required not to trigger a lot of questions that would make the rounds of the hospitality community in New Orleans. He would never want to embarrass Anne in front of her contemporaries, nor did he have any desire for word of his tinkering with fate to get back to her.

Damn it, if she'd just accept a simple, businesslike loan, he wouldn't have to tread such a precarious path.

Of course, none of what was between them had anything to do with business. And it wasn't the least bit simple.

Judith had seen through to the heart of him. If this were any other hotel, he'd be snapping it up with merciless speed. He'd built a thriving chain by having an instinct for timing, efficiency and economy, leveraging himself into putting out the least investment for the greatest return.

He would never have believed the day would come when he'd be guilty of anything as senseless as making this offer.

Much less enjoying the prospect so much. Despite the potential for disaster, it had been a long time since he had danced this close to the razor's edge.

The woman was making him crazy.

And he was having a ball.

CHAPTER EIGHT

"CORBIN," THE VOICE RASPED. "Clock is ticking. Your note comes due in ten days."

"You'll get your hotel," Dan Corbin said. "And our debt will be erased."

"Maybe."

Maybe? If he were his reckless brother Richard, he'd be blustering threats, scattering shotgun bursts of defiance.

Thank the fates that crime boss Mike Blount only had Dan's cell number. This situation called for a clear head. "Our arrangement was clear. In exchange for the funds to pay off the note coming due on our Lafayette property, we deed the Hotel Marchand to you as soon as we close on it. You get your foothold in the Quarter, a respectable front to expand your gambling operation plus some high-class whores operating out of a few of the rooms. Everybody wins."

"Your boy inside isn't getting the job done."

Dan had his own reservations about Luc Carter, but he wasn't sharing them with this man. "He's had a few setbacks."

"He ain't got jack accomplished."

"The hotel's bookings are not where they should be.

This is their biggest season, and they're losing ground. They know they're not gonna make it. I just upped the ante. The mother will cave."

"Not if Regency Corp. steps in."

Regency Corp.? Oh, hell. "They won't," he bluffed. "Not their kind of property."

"Anne Marchand has been spending a lot of time with William Armstrong." A pause. "You didn't know that, did you?"

Dan silently muttered vile curses. "Of course I did. It's not what you think. Armstrong and her husband hated each other." Why hadn't Carter told him about this?

"Then what was she doing having dinner with him last night? Or in a lip-lock with him this morning?"

The bastard had someone watching Anne Marchand. Looking over Dan's shoulders.

Bluster wouldn't get past this. Only action would. "I'm stepping up the pace. I'm thinking a good fire will be the killing blow." He'd already placed a call to Carter, who, damn him, wasn't answering.

"I don't want my property damaged."

"Done properly, serious damage will be minimal, but the revenues the Marchand women are counting on to save them will be history."

"Who you got planning the logistics?"

"A couple of guys who know their stuff." Or he would have.

"My guys are better. I'll have Ricky and Hank call you."

Everywhere Dan looked, the walls were closing in.

Damn Richard for playing fast and loose with the money they'd socked away. Once this was over, he was going solo.

For now, though, he had to keep his head and get himself out of this problem. He'd cut his brother loose gladly, except that it was better to keep him close, so he could limit further damage. "That would be great. Thanks."

"Don't thank me," Blount said. "Get me my hotel or get me the money…and the interest just went up ten per cent."

Dan squeezed the bridge of his nose. "You won't need the interest. The Hotel Marchand will be mine by Mardi Gras, and yours soon after."

"Unless you get extradited before then, you dumbshit. You and your brother committed the one un-forgivable sin that will take down a con every time."

Dan clenched his jaw. "And what was that?" *You sanctimonious prick.*

"Not knowing when to get out. You got greedy."

"No one knows where we are." Though he was damned tired of being on the lam.

"I do." Blount laughed. "Easiest thing in the world to drop a dime on you."

"But you won't. You need me."

"For now."

The call ended with a decisive click.

LUC'S PHONE VIBRATED in his pocket. He ignored it as he soothed a distraught woman whose luggage had been lost by the airlines and who needed a dress for a special occasion tonight. "Monique will take superb care of you, Mrs. Davis. Her boutique caters to the cream of New Orleans." He punched in the numbers of A Private Affair.

"But my clothes always need alteration, and the dinner is three hours from now." The woman's eyes were red. "Frank told me not to pack so much that I had to check a bag, but I was just so afraid I wouldn't have the right clothes. This promotion is so important to him."

"I promise you—" The smoky voice answered. "Monique? It's Luc Carter at the Marchand."

His cell vibrated again, and Luc tried to tune it out, along with the sniffles from their guest as he related what he needed to Monique.

The days were insane, and they were only going to get worse as Carnival heated up. This job was a killer, even without the additional pressures exerted by the Corbins.

He frowned at the thought, and Mrs. Davis began to weep again. "Oh, no. I knew it."

"No, no. Everything is fine." Into the phone he said, "Twenty minutes would be wonderful, Monique."

He hung up and focused on their guest, though his cell was vibrating again. "If you'll return to your room, Mrs. Davis, Monique will be here in about twenty minutes with a selection of gowns from which you can choose."

The woman looked as if she'd just seen Santa Claus. "She will?" Then her brow wrinkled. "But what if they don't fit?"

"Monique is an accomplished seamstress herself, and she has another one on her staff. She promises you will be dressed to kill this evening. If your husband doesn't get promoted, it won't be because his wife wasn't suitably attired."

The woman launched herself at him and caught him in a death grip. "Oh, Mr. Carter—" She gave him a big, smacking kiss on the cheek. "You're just— I don't know what I'd have done." She was weeping again.

Luc patted her on the back and gently removed her. He took one hand and pressed it between his. "The Hotel Marchand takes pride in the tender care of its guests. It was my privilege to help you." He removed the snowy handkerchief that he'd learned to carry in this job, one of a stack always waiting in his office. "Please." He held it out to her. "And perhaps you would allow me to send our masseuse to your suite, once Monique has finished?" Anne Marchand had been very smart to allow a massage therapist space to set up shop here, for situations just like this.

"Oh, my word, you are just the loveliest man," she said, blowing her nose. Her head lifted. "Are you married? My daughter is so sweet, and she—"

"Of course she is. And it's easy to see why, with a beautiful mother like you." Gently he turned her and escorted her toward the elevator. When the doors opened, he ushered her inside. "Have a lovely evening, Mrs. Davis."

The woman's eyes sparkled with hope for the first time. "Oh, I can't thank you enough, Mr. Carter. Why, I—" She was still talking as the doors closed.

"I was so concerned that we'd never find a suitable replacement for Alphonse," said a low, beautifully-modulated voice from behind him. "But he couldn't possibly have handled that better."

Luc turned to face Anne Marchand. Felt again the wash of shame at what had been done to her and her daughters. Her hotel. "Thank you."

"If you decide to marry Mrs. Davis's daughter, please promise me you'll make her come live in New Orleans." Anne smiled, but Luc saw a glimmer of her worry. "We need you, Luc. It's going to require all of us to get this hotel on safe ground."

Just then, Luc's phone vibrated again, and it was all he could do not to hurl it to the floor. "I'm happy to be part of the team," he said, and meant it. Somehow he would make this up to her.

"Part of the family," she insisted.

He'd never really experienced that. It had been only him and his mother for so long.

Anne didn't know what she was saying or how her words were water on dry, thirsty ground.

Though he had no right, he smiled back at her. "Family." He wanted to offer her something now, some sign of hope. "We'll make it, Mrs. Marchand. What you've built will still be here for your grandchildren and their children."

If he'd felt bad before, he felt worse now as her beautiful eyes swam with tears. She pressed one hand to his forearm. "My girls need you, Luc. Thank you so much for being here." She paused, studied him, her gaze warmer than ever, but sad, too.

"What is it?"

She shook her head. "Nothing, just…" She laughed

faintly. "For a second there, you reminded me of someone I haven't seen in a long time. I love him very much."

He frowned. "Who is it?"

She bit her lip. "My brother."

Luc's heart started pounding in double time. "I didn't know you have a brother," he all but stammered.

"I don't know if I still do or not. He's been gone for many, many years, but I still miss him." She pinched her nose. "Don't mind me. Just an old woman's folly."

"You're not old."

"You're sweet," she said. "He was a troubled boy, but he was sweet, too, with me. I loved him desperately and tried to protect him, but—" She waved a hand. "I apologize. You're busy, and I must be on my way, too. Thank you again for all your hard work, Luc. Remy would have been so pleased with you."

Desperately, Luc wanted to prolong the conversation, but this was not the place or the time.

And she would hate him when she knew.

As he was beginning to hate himself.

So he watched her go, sobered by the knowledge of just how wrong he'd been about everyone but his termagant of a grandmother.

Anne had loved her brother. Missed him still.

I'm so sorry, he wanted to say to the woman walking away from him. *I'll make it up to you, I swear.*

His phone vibrated again.

Jaw clenched, he yanked it from his pocket and answered. "Carter."

"Where the hell have you been?" Dan Corbin shouted. "Why aren't you answering?"

Luc bit back the retort jostling to be said. "I have a job."

"To hell with that. You work for me."

Screw this. "I'm doing my best," he managed.

"It's not good enough."

Corbin sounded frantic. "What's wrong?"

"What's wrong? He asks me what's wrong?" Corbin's voice rose. "We have ten days until Mardi Gras, and that bitch isn't budging. It's time to up the ante."

"How?"

"I want you to find the best place to start a fire."

Luc's blood chilled. "You can't mean that."

"I do."

"A fire could kill someone. And in the Quarter, everything is too close together. It could be a nightmare. Why would you want to damage the hotel? That hurts you, too."

"I didn't ask your opinion. Anyway, I've got experts coming in. We don't want major damage, just some added pressure. Some smoke, enough stuff burned to send guests home, shut down the hotel during the busiest season."

"Then you'd have to restore their confidence when you take over. Why would you want to do that?"

"You don't question my orders, Carter. You just take them, or—"

"Or what?"

"You're not doing the job, you're no use to us." The menace was unmistakable.

Luc had never encountered anything like this. For a

second, he was tempted to run. He could get a job anywhere.

But there was his aunt. His cousins. Family.

He had no choice but to stay here and be alert. He'd have to be everywhere. All the time. Christ, it was impossible—

"You hear me, Carter? I'll give you one day to figure out where to set the fire, then I'm sending in a team. They have a lot of skills besides arson." The threat was clear. He played along or he was gone… maybe permanently.

If only he had someone he could talk to. Bounce ideas off. *Dear God, Papa. What have I done?*

He had to buy time to think, but time was in short supply. Very short.

"I hear you."

"Good."

Then Corbin was gone.

WILLIAM LEFT Jud Lawson's office, satisfied with the offer they'd structured. Jud had assured him that his staff would have the documents in proper form by noon, and Jud would deliver the offer to Charlotte Marchand himself.

In his heart, William wanted to hand them to Anne, not Charlotte, and in person. To tender the offer as proof that he would do anything, whatever it took, to secure her future. To be sure she understood his motivation.

But he already knew that she would, at best, tear up the documents with a pitying smile.

At worst, she'd snap the fragile link between them

and refuse to see him ever again. Then he'd be power-less to protect her.

This approach, while risky, was the best compro-mise he could structure. He could always recant on the offer, should she and Charlotte accept it, once the hotel was back on its feet. Or deed the hotel back to her, if the future he was beginning to hope for panned out but she didn't want to be business partners.

In the meantime, the offer would be there and, best he could ascertain from his sources, significantly higher than the one Anne was wrestling with now—but not so high that it would be immediately suspect. It would serve as a placeholder, a fallback position to give Anne heart.

But because it was made through Jud as trustee, it bore no connection to William. He could continue as her confidant. Stay close and be privy to what she was thinking. Free to intervene, if needed.

He pulled into the parking garage at his office, feeling easier than he had in weeks. Months, actually. He was not a man well-suited to inaction. Maybe this wasn't the ideal solution, but given Anne's stubborn pride, it was the best he could manage. He was incapable of simply standing back and watching her struggle any longer while doing nothing himself. She'd already wound up in the hospital from the combined weight of worry and work.

She was too important to him, and he was not going to take a chance on losing her.

For a second, his thoughts lingered on the woman who'd greeted him at his door this morning, eyes dark with concern, off-balance yet determinedly offering an apology.

And the woman who'd all but kissed his socks off. Laughed with him. Teased him.

Taunted him with possibilities….

There was no maybe to it, he saw now. He was captivated by Anne Marchand.

Crazy in love with her.

He was grinning as the elevator doors opened. Still grinning as his receptionist, then his assistant smiled back.

"Daddy," Judith called from behind him.

He turned. "Hi, sweetheart."

"Wow. What's put that gleam in your eye?" Then her face fell. "I imagine I could guess."

He resisted a sigh. Real life was often overrated, he decided. Daydreaming was much more fun. "How are you doing today?" he asked instead.

She brightened. Brandished a sheaf of papers. "Here— this is for you. Glen and I finished late last night, but I wanted to look it over one more time before I showed you."

He took the papers. "What is it?" Afraid he knew.

Her glow dimmed a bit, but she stood straight and tall, resembling, he suspected, no one more than himself. "It's an outline of the offer for the Hotel Marchand."

"Honey, I—"

"You said you'd look at it. It makes total sense and could be a great deal for Regency." Her expression was both ruthless and earnest. Shaky pride and a touch of defiance.

He'd be churlish to reject it out of hand. "All right." He bought time. "It may not be today, though. I have a full slate of meetings."

Disappointment chased over her features. "Tomorrow, then. Unless you get extra time today. Or tonight."

He'd be with Anne tonight, but that probably wasn't the best news he could deliver at the moment. His heart went out to his wounded child, who was struggling to make a fresh start. To make him proud of her; it wasn't her fault she'd chosen a project with a terrible conflict inherent in it.

He found a smile for her. "You've worked hard on this."

"I don't mind hard work, Daddy. You've provided an excellent example of what can come of it." She looked shy as a fawn, and the years suddenly fell away. *Daddy, I got my report card, and see the As? Daddy, would you come watch my Christmas program?*

He had tried, but the very demands of that example she was touting had meant that he'd missed more of her growing up than he would have liked. But Isabel had been there for all of it, and he'd told himself that they made a great team, that through both of them, their daughter had all she needed.

Now Judith had no marriage, no children and no mother. Only him.

"I promise I'll get to it at the first opportunity." Though how on earth he would let her down easy was beyond him at the moment.

Then inspiration hit. If he expanded her arena of opportunities, maybe this offer wouldn't be so important to her. "Honey, I wonder if you'd be interested in a new project, one I'd really like your take on."

He saw pride transform her. "What is it?"

"Are you free to make a trip in my place? To the Dallas property?"

She nodded. "How soon?"

"Tomorrow, if you could manage. The day after, if not."

"Of course. What is it you need from me?"

He indicated his office with his head. "Come on in, and I'll get you up to speed on it."

There was a spring to her step that he hadn't seen since her return. He acknowledged to himself that shifting her attention was his initial motivation, and postponing the urgency to respond on this offer she'd drafted wasn't far behind.

But he was also becoming more impressed by the day at the woman Judith could be when not bowed down by the failure of her marriage or searching for a new direction in her life.

She was heir to all that he'd built, and she was a smart woman. She'd wanted to build a separate life before, but now she was here. She could choose to own the company and let others run it, but if she discovered that she wanted to do more than deposit her checks, he would be a happy man.

"I love you, sweetheart," he said.

The smile she cast at him was brilliant. "I love you, too, Daddy."

He followed her inside.

"MAMA?"

Anne looked up quickly, caught by the concern in Charlotte's tone. She pitched her voice low so only Charlotte could hear. "Are you all right?"

"Yes. No." Charlotte shook her head. "Maybe. Do you have a second to talk?"

"Of course." Anne abandoned the napkins she'd been folding while chatting with the waitstaff. Over the years, she'd discovered that she learned much more about the operational details of the hotel by getting down in the trenches with her staff than by reading all the reports in the world. She'd been able to head off many a problem by doing so, and the time spent always seemed to boost the morale of the staff. Her manner and bearing could convey a confidence that spoke louder than all the pep talks in meetings she could hold. The hotel employee grapevine could be an owner's greatest asset—or a bane. Rumors spread faster than an internet virus, and she knew that recent events in the hotel had everyone concerned.

Charlotte was doing a great job—all her daughters were—but they were also strapped for time and working far too hard, especially her eldest. Actions like this were a small, quiet way Anne could appear to be doing nothing taxing while making a difference, however slight.

And these were her people, still. Some of them had been with her since the beginning, but even the newest employee had always been greeted by Anne Marchand. Babies and marriages celebrated, family losses mourned.

No hotel management course would advise this, but it had worked for Anne for years and still would.

"Luisa, I'm sorry, but duty calls," Anne said to the pregnant waitress beside her. "You stay off your feet for a while longer."

"Yes, Mrs. Marchand. I swear I'm feeling fine."

"Good." Anne patted her hand. "We want to keep you that way. See you later, everyone."

Farewells came from all of them. Anne waved and followed her daughter, who stopped outside and faced her.

"You are amazing, you know that?"

Anne did a double take. "Why, thank you, *chère*."

"No, I mean it. You are the heart and soul of this hotel. You've done my job and still managed time for—" she pointed back to the restaurant "—that. And so much else that it's requiring all four of us to step into your place." Charlotte shoved a hand through her dark hair. "And you raised four children. I'm single, no kids, and I'm—"

For a second, Charlotte looked as though she would cry, something very out of character.

"Oh, honey, you're exhausted." At Charlotte's impatient shake of her head, Anne persisted. "Come with me."

"Where?" A far cry from normal, Charlotte allowed herself to be urged along.

"My quarters. You need to put your feet up. Have a good cry."

That her headstrong, always-together daughter only made a token refusal worried Anne more than anything else could. She remained silent until they were safely inside her apartment. "Sit down, *doucette*. I'll make us some tea."

"You should have been *une anglaise,* Mama." Charlotte's laugh was a little shaky. "It isn't French to drink so much tea."

"You're surviving on coffee," Anne responded as she

put water in the kettle. "And anyway, tea is all I know how to make."

Her daughter's amusement wasn't forced this time. "Papa tried to teach you to cook. I remember."

Anne turned on the burner. Remy had insisted that he needed at least a small kitchen in their quarters, though he had everything he could want downstairs. "Yes, and the only reason we remained married was that he finally accepted that it was impossible." She readied the teapot and cups, then crossed to her daughter. "Now what's this about? You are doing a magnificent job, Charlotte, and your circumstances are far different than mine were."

"You built this place, Mama. When everyone thought you'd fail. How can that not be harder than what I'm facing?"

"*Exactement.* We had nowhere to go but up, your papa and I. And I didn't build this place myself. I had him, and we were young, and…" Memories flooded over her, but she shook her head and focused on her child. "It was very different, that's all. We grew into what this place is. Holding on when you're at the top is always harder. Even without all the little disasters that have erupted so close together." She patted Charlotte's knee. "Oh, *bébé,* I am so sorry you must carry the weight of this on your shoulders. I'm feeling fine. You must allow me to resume more of my former duties."

"So I can feel even less competent because even with my sisters helping, I still can't get the job done?"

Anne ignored the whistling kettle. "You *are* getting

the job done. And your sisters are only replacing employees we already had." She had to remember that Charlotte despised weakness in herself and resisted any form of pity. "I still believe a good cry would do you a world of good, but if you're determined to refuse, then—" She rose to silence the boiling water.

"We have another offer."

Anne's hand froze on the burner knob. "What?" She removed the kettle by rote and busied herself warming the pot, then spooning tea leaves inside and adding water. "*Les cochons* backed down or threatened us further?" She utilized the unflattering term they'd tagged on the odious Corbin brothers.

"Neither. This is a whole new offer from another party."

Anne understood why Charlotte's voice was flat. This meant that news of their straits had gotten out. The feeding frenzy would begin. She kept her own voice carefully neutral. "From whom?"

"I don't know. It's in the name of a trustee."

"A competitor, then." Using a trustee to ensure anonymity was a common practice to give the buyer an advantage, because the seller couldn't ascribe motives or negotiate based on knowledge of the buyer's situation, its strengths or weaknesses. "How bad is it?"

"That's the problem. It's a good offer. Not generous, but fair."

"I see." Anne lifted the tray and carried the tea service to the coffee table. "Good enough you think we should accept it?"

"Oh, Mama." Charlotte's eyes were much younger

than her years now, and aching. "I don't know." She glanced away. "I just keep wondering what Papa would say…." She was silent for endless moments. Then she looked back at Anne, and a single tear crept down her cheek. "He'd be so disappointed in me. I promised him once that if anything ever happened to him, I'd take care of you. Now—" Her hand fluttered ineffectually.

Anne set the tray down with a thud. "Remy Marchand, if you were here now…" She put her hands on her hips. "I could strangle the man. He had no right to place that burden on you. I am perfectly capable of—"

"He loved you, Mama. Worshipped the ground you walked on."

The truth took the wind from her sails. "I adored him, too," she murmured. "So much so that the heart was torn out of me when he died." She'd gone on because she had to, had grown a skin over the bleeding ache, turned a soft crab shell into bones. Slowly found an echo of joy where she'd once known blazing rapture.

It was a shock to realize that she was heart-whole again. Thanks to William.

Another shock to know that her first impulse was to tell William about this latest offer. Use him as a backboard to bounce ideas off, until she could settle in her own mind what was the right thing to do.

The whole notion was disturbing. And wonderful.

She'd ponder that. Later. For now, she had a daughter to care for. With a new strength that she understood derived at least in part from knowing she wasn't alone if she didn't want to be anymore, she sat up straighter.

"Tell me the details." She placed one hand on her daughter's. "We'll get through this, I promise. And whatever we decide will be fine with your father. I'm not the only one he adored, you know."

Charlotte sniffed, then accepted the tissue Anne proffered. Blew her nose quietly. "Okay." She reached for her teacup. "Okay, here's the deal."

And she began to talk.

CHAPTER NINE

WILLIAM WALKED INTO the Hotel Marchand and saw it with new eyes. Conflicted ones.

"Good evening, Mr. Armstrong. May I ring Mrs. Marchand for you?" the concierge asked. The greeting couldn't be faulted, warm and welcoming, yet with a clear note to William that eyes were watching, that Anne was a treasure to be guarded.

He cast a quick glance at the name tag. "Luc, is it?"

A nod. "Luc Carter, sir. At your service."

With a newly awakened consciousness, thanks to his daughter's very thorough report, he noted items that even his veteran hotelier's scrutiny had skimmed over— recent visits here had been all about his interest in Anne and not the tiny details that made the difference between a good hotel and great one.

Intelligent, engaged employees—check.

A faultless first impression—check. Anne's touch was everywhere, in the warm gold walls, the intriguing mix of French and Spanish antiques with cushy sofas and chairs in shades of cream and red. Lush greenery dotted the inside and grew thick and full in the courtyard. Elegance and comfort, grace and welcome, reflecting the woman herself.

"Sir?" Carter asked, still patiently waiting in the manner of a superb concierge. As if he had all the time in the world for your smallest wish, even if he were juggling a killer load of demands.

"She's expecting me, but if procedure demands that you call her first, please feel free."

Luc smiled and picked up the phone. "Thank you, sir. Only a matter of routine."

William caught the faintest flicker of concern in the man's expression. Given the chain of small and not-so-small disasters that had plagued this hotel, William could only be grateful for Luc's cordial insistence. "Certainly."

Luc's call was answered and, after a brief exchange, ended. "Mrs. Marchand asks you to come up." His eyes twinkled. "And in her own gracious way, she encouraged me not to bother you with this procedure again."

William had to grin. "That's my Anne. Could tell off the devil himself and make it sound like an invitation to high tea."

Luc smothered his own smile. "Yes, sir. Have a good evening, sir."

William saluted with the bouquet of lilacs he'd had flown in just this afternoon. "Thank you."

"Luc!" A woman in her late forties with a figure tending toward the Rubenesque crossed the foyer and left the arms of her escort to twirl right in front of Luc's desk. "Look! See what your amazing Monique did?"

"Mrs. Davis." Smoothly, he clasped her hand and bowed over it. "You are a vision."

"Frank, this is the young man I told you about. He saved me." She was a dervish, whirling back toward Luc. "Frank got the promotion this afternoon, as it turns out. We're celebrating with his new boss tonight, and my luggage still hasn't arrived. You are an angel, Luc. An absolute angel."

"I was happy to help," Luc demurred. "Mr. Davis, may I offer my congratulations?"

"Thanks. And thanks for what you did for her. She can't stop raving about the massage the hotel supplied." He grinned. "That dress cost me a pretty penny, but it's worth it. Looks like the girl I married."

"We want our guests to feel pampered."

"Worried about the price before we came, I have to admit," the man grumbled.

"But we'll be back, Frank, won't we?" Mrs. Davis trilled.

"Good place," her husband acknowledged.

"And I've already called half my friends to tell them what you did for me," she said.

Customers who want to return—check. Who are made to feel special.

William kept going toward the elevator. The signs of wear were subtle but creeping in. An infusion of cash was needed, no question.

But Anne still had a jewel here, even if its setting was slightly tarnished. His hotels were smoothly-run and excellent values, but all of them were huge, designed to capitalize on economies of scale.

His daughter was right—and wrong. Combining this hotel with his would be more efficient, true.

But the Hotel Marchand was unique, and any encroachment into the magic Anne—and Remy, he conceded, but mostly Anne—had created would eat at the core of what made the place special.

When he was younger, he'd been bent on more and bigger. At this point in his life, he'd learned the value of a quiet gem: a moment of peace, a touch of dew on a flower. A small, exquisite painting or a good bottle of wine he'd never heard of before.

A woman like Anne. Except there was no *like*. She was one of a kind, a pearl beyond price.

He was surprised to realize, as he approached her door, that he was…nervous.

When was the last time he'd felt that odd jitter? When something had been important enough that he feared losing it?

Amazing. And…fun.

Then Anne opened her door, and all his musings ground to a halt.

"Hi," she said. "Oh! Lilacs." She reached out, and he surrendered them.

Along with his heart.

IN THE MINUTES between Luc's call and William's arrival, Anne had considered yet another change of clothing. She could no longer remember what had made her so bold this morning. Couldn't feel that tug of heat, sweet and potent, that had nearly landed her in William's bed in broad daylight.

She was too old for this. Not a phrase—or a mindset—she favored, but completely appropriate, nonetheless.

It was too late for plastic surgery or a girdle. Too—

Terrifying. She was petrified of what she might have promised without using the words. Of the expectations he would bring to the evening. She wasn't ready. Would never be ready to get naked with a new man.

She had been on her way to the phone to beg Luc to fend off William, to proffer an excuse because she was—

A tap on her door.

A coward, after all.

I can't date, I can't date, I can't—

Then she'd opened the door to lilacs.

"Oh!" She bent to sniff the blossoms, fragrant with their sweet, flirty scent. "Where on earth did you find them? I swear they're the best smell on earth. I'd only read about them before I went to college further north, and then—"

"Hello, Anne." With a smile, William bent to kiss her, and she turned just enough that his kiss landed on her cheek. "You look amazing." He scanned the lines of the scarlet silk sheath she was certain she should have bought for Charlotte instead of herself.

"Oh. Well, I—" She turned away. "I'll just get these in water." She put distance between them as fast as possible.

"May I come in?" he asked from the doorway.

Oh, sweet heaven. What was she doing? "Of course.

I'm sorry. I—" She glanced up and met his cheery gaze. She narrowed her eyes. "Don't you stand there and be amused at me."

His eyebrows rose. "All right." He entered. Closed the door quietly.

She found a vase. Put the flowers in water. Focused on each stem as if the fate of the world depended on its placement.

"How was your day?" he asked, coming toward her.

She stepped sideways. "Fine."

"Anne, what's wrong?"

"Nothing." But the concern in his voice nearly broke her. She'd put on a brave face for Charlotte, but all afternoon, she'd been arguing with herself as she went about her activities. Looking at every aspect of the hotel and wondering how she would ever say goodbye when she had memories attached to every square inch, every single person.

One stalk broke. "Oh, *merde*—" She dropped the rest of them on the counter as she battled the urge to cry. "William, I don't think I'm able to do this." She steadied her tone. "Perhaps we could reschedule or—"

Hands settled on her shoulders. Turned her. "Come here," he said in a voice so warm and comforting that she couldn't find it in her to resist, though it changed nothing.

Then his arms came around her, and he pulled her into his chest.

It felt wonderful, but she held part of herself back, knowing the next step would be for him to demand that she explain, and even though she was almost certain he would understand at least part of her agony, he wouldn't know the worst of it, that she, not Charlotte, had failed and would lose, for all of them, the place that was not just a business or a livelihood—

But a home. Their home, the only one the girls had known. And their history, the one Remy had hoped would endure for generations.

Remy's mark on the world, erased. It was a letting-go of him nearly as cruel as watching that coffin slide into the crypt. Remy and his legacy would live on only in their hearts, while others would forget all too soon.

But William surprised her. He didn't ask anything. Say anything.

He only held her. A refuge she shouldn't accept, didn't deserve.

He bent his head to hers. "Hey," he whispered. "Want me to cancel our reservations?"

She turned her face to the side but slid her arms around his waist. "Yes. No."

She tried to draw away, but he wouldn't let her. "Shh, it's okay. They'll hold the table if you'd like to think about it awhile."

They probably would. One of the perks of power. She leaned back, met his scrutiny. "I don't know what I want. Maybe you should just go. Call someone else."

He smiled only slightly. "I threw away my little black book."

She could drown in those blue eyes. "That might not have been wise. Have the garbage men come yet?"

He laughed then.

"It's not funny. I have no idea what I'm doing."

"It doesn't matter. Just hang on to me for now. You don't have to decide anything or be anything but yourself."

"I'm sixty-two years old, and I changed clothes four times this evening. I still haven't found the right outfit."

He scanned her without letting her go. Waggled his eyebrows. "Looks good to me."

"What's underneath won't." Then she sucked in a breath of horror that she'd said it aloud.

To his credit, he didn't laugh. Instead, he picked up one hand and laced their fingers. "Would it help you to know that I nearly didn't show?"

"Really?"

He smiled. "No."

When she tried to yank her hand away, he only tightened his grip and kissed the pad of her thumb. She inhaled sharply, and he nipped lightly with his teeth, then grazed a path down to the mound at its base.

She felt it all the way to her insides, as though he'd hit on a direct connection. She couldn't quite stifle a tiny moan. "William, I'm serious."

Heated breath crept over her palm. She wanted to yank her hand away. Wanted more to savor the warmth spreading from one tiny patch of flesh into the furthest recesses of her body.

"So am I." The vibration of his voice sent more ripples over her skin.

Dear, sweet heaven.

He bent to the inside of her elbow. One slow drag of his tongue over the tenderest part had her breath hitching.

"I'm not playing," she protested.

He crooked her a grin. "Too bad. I am." He straightened, only to lean again, this time with his mouth brushing the pulse point at her neck.

My heart pounded, books always said. Had it ever been quite like this?

Then suddenly, he straightened. Stepped back, still holding her hand. "Ready for dinner?" he asked with the tone of a lazy tiger, if one could talk. "Or shall we order in?"

"What?"

His smile was both tease and temptation. "Are you hungry?"

"For what?"

His laugh was a little strained. "If you don't want me making love to you this second," he said as he drew her toward the door, "we have to go. Now."

She followed, still trying to get her legs to function, all the while wondering if food was that important. "Okay. If you think we should."

He whirled on her then, and those blue eyes weren't laughing anymore. They were dark as navy. "What I think is that we should climb in bed for a solid week and tell the world to go stuff itself. But since Mardi Gras is ten days away, and you would never forgive yourself, I'll settle for postponing. Barely."

"Oh." Her head was still a little light. "Of course, you're right. We have no business going to bed together with so much else going on." All too quickly, reality flooded in. "As a matter of fact, maybe I should just stay." She wheeled and focused on the remaining lilacs.

"I didn't say postpone making love, darling. Only the solid week of it."

"Um—" She stabbed in the last stalk, finding herself with equal parts relief and fascination.

"Forgot to worry about what was under your clothes for a few minutes there, didn't you?" He grinned. "Making love is about more than skin, sweetheart, though I do have an appetite for more of yours."

"Oh." She was beginning to sound like a broken record. "No lights," she insisted.

He winked at her. "We'll negotiate over dinner." He tugged at her hand. "I'll warn you that I'm reputed to be quite a shark."

"I knew that." Her stomach fluttered. "I'm not so bad myself," she said.

Whistling her way past the graveyard.

"THIS IS WONDERFUL," Anne said. She touched the heavy silver, trailed her fingers over the blush-pink linen. Glanced around at their fellow diners and up to the ornate chandeliers as if she hadn't experienced such luxury often in her life. "Another find of yours." She smiled at him. "I can't recall the last time I went even this far for dinner." She shook her head. "As though Metairie were across the planet and not right next door."

"It had never occurred to me before that you didn't dine out all the time. Check out the competition."

"Hardly. With Remy's hands-on approach and the demands of four children…"

"And the little matter of a hotel to run," he offered. "I never cease to be amazed at all you've juggled, Anne." He picked up her hand. Nibbled on her fingers. "You've been the poster girl for having it all."

"Not really." A delightful bit of color rose into her cheeks.

"I have no idea where you got the energy, yet you made it look effortless."

"I spent years dreaming of a week to do nothing but sleep." She made a joke of it.

He wasn't buying. "You got your wish a few months ago in the hospital. Scared the hell out of me."

Her eyes popped open. "You?"

"You'd been under enormous pressure. Like all of New Orleans, I had wondered what would happen after Remy's accident."

She removed her hand—or tried to.

His grip tightened. "No disrespect to you intended, Anne. I understood better than most what would be required for the hotel to continue as it had been. Remy was a genius in the kitchen, and the restaurant was a draw as much to residents as to hotel guests. You had your hands full already, and you were grieving."

Her gaze darkened. "I barely remember those days. For months, all I could do was just get up each morning and put one foot in front of the other."

"I understand."

"I know you do."

"But I had it easier. I was accustomed to being the sole force behind my business. You had lost not only a mate but a partner." He turned her hand over and stared at her palm. "Anne, it would be disingenuous of me to deny that once I would have enjoyed getting the best of Remy." He glanced up. "But as competitors in a fair fight. I never wished you any harm, and I would not have seen you go through that for anything."

"I believe you."

"I watched you pick up the entire burden, and I was all too aware that the odds of your making it were not strong."

"And now they've caught up with me," she said, seeming unutterably weary and sad.

"No." Here was one more thing he could do for her. Bolster her spirits. "I've seen you in action. You are a force to be reckoned with, Anne Marchand."

Her pleased surprise said his judgment was sound.

"I won't say I don't worry, though" he confessed. "You landed in a hospital bed not that long ago. I wish—"

Now it was she who gripped his hand. "I appreciate that you want to help, William. I do." Her voice wavered, and she pressed her lips together, staring at the tablecloth.

Then her gaze rose. "You have no idea what it means to know that you'll stand back and let me fight my own battles."

A stake through the heart. The war inside him, quiet for a bit, heated up once more. He wrestled with his conscience and his need to shield a woman becoming increasingly precious. "Anne—"

She held up a hand. "I don't kid myself that you like doing it, but I can't possibly express the strength it gives me to know that you will. Even more, that you're there. That you care."

"I do." If he conveyed nothing else to her, this was paramount. If he was making a mistake, there was no malice in it. He subdued the unrest inside him, deciding to have faith that she would understand, once she knew what he'd done. "Anne, I do care. Probably more than you're comfortable with yet."

She smiled. "You might be surprised. I am." Before he could respond, she continued. "You're right. Something did happen today. Are you up for listening?"

"Of course. Would you care for coffee while we're talking?"

A quick shake of her head. "I'm fine." A quicker curve of lips. "But I might want to make you some at my place."

The suggestion in her eyes made his heart skip. "I have a cake Estelle made at my place."

"A new twist on 'want to see my etchings?'"

He twirled an imaginary mustache. "Do you?"

Her laughter gave him hope. Keeping a firm grasp on the hand he'd been holding nonstop since dinner, he lifted the other to catch their waiter and signal for the check. "Okay," he said. "Talk to me."

"We have another offer for the hotel. From a new party."

The squeeze of his fingers was involuntary. "Who is it?"

Her mouth turned down. "A trustee, so it has to be a competitor, seeking to disguise their true identity."

This was hard. So hard. "Any guesses?"

She shook her head. "We haven't gotten that far. Charlotte was devastated."

"Why?"

"This means word has gotten out that we're in trouble. The vultures will be circling." She sighed. "We almost have to take it because it's a decent offer, and if we don't snap it up, it will likely go away as soon as the other offers begin to come in."

He frowned. "There's no—" He cleared his throat. "Is there a time limit on it?"

"No, and that's odd. Probably just means it's not a local entity, but word spreads."

Damn it, he'd meant to ease her mind, not burden it. "Would it be so wrong to accept the offer? You said the terms are generous."

"I'll probably have to, but—" She rubbed her forehead. "Doing so will mean saying goodbye to Remy's dream. To Charlotte's future. Oh, the money will allow me to set each of the girls up, as well as take care of myself if I'm careful—"

"Anne, I want to—" He signed the check, all but shoved it at the waiter. "Damn it, I want to take care of you. You don't have to worry about that anymore."

She blinked at him. "What are you saying?"

The alarm in her tone had him scrambling for footing. It was not a sensation he was accustomed to. And definitely didn't like. "I'm in love with you." He paused, jutted his chin. "Go ahead. Run away from it. I know you want to." He shoved to his feet. "I'll take you home."

"Wait, wait." She put her face in her hands. "I can't keep up with you."

"Well, speed up," he ordered. "Or tell me to go to the devil and leave you alone."

"Would you sit down?" she hissed. "I didn't say I didn't want to catch up, just—"

Elegant Anne, hissing. In public. He almost smiled. If he weren't so off-balance and sure he'd just screwed up everything he'd driven himself nuts holding back from, he'd laugh.

"Please." She looked up at him.

He was out of practice at backing down. About fifty years out of practice.

But she'd said *please*. And, damn it, he loved her. So he sat. "You're driving me insane, you know that?"

"Well, join the club," she snapped.

First hissing, now snapping. He did laugh then. Leaned across the table and caught her gaze. "Which of us, do you suppose, is the most out of their element?"

Her lips twitched, and the hazel eyes warmed again. "I've been the soul of rationality for so many years."

"Yeah. Me, too." His laughter was a shout this time. "I thought I was settled now. Ready to ride slowly into the sunset."

She snorted. "Get real."

Snorting now, his Anne. *His* Anne. Good heaven, she made him feel alive again, his world wide with possibilities. "Want to ditch this place?" He tilted one eyebrow. "See just how slowly I can ride?"

The sudden darkening of her pupils told him all he

needed to know. "I think I just might," she answered, and the huskiness went straight to his gut.

He rose, grabbed her hand, drew her to him. "Come on. Let's blow this joint."

He tucked her under his arm and resolved to do whatever was required to keep her this close forever.

She snuggled into him as they walked into a night filled with stars.

I WANT TO take care of you. I love you.

Dangerous words, those. Her head was spinning, and it wasn't from two glasses of wine, however excellent. All the way to his house—he hadn't asked again but just set his course—they rode in silence. As if to speak one word might fracture the fragile thread spinning between them, though its girth seemed wider by the moment, its heft more daunting. She had the ineluctable sense that this night, they had crossed—or would cross—a boundary, and returning to the safety of her known world would be nigh unto impossible.

Not that her world seemed all that safe, at the moment. But it was familiar. Held a history and a place she knew how to inhabit.

William might be older, but he was no less the buccaneer than in his youth. At least not with her. His single-minded pursuit was both intoxicating and slightly alarming. But flattering, oh yes, indeed. Nearly enough to make her forget the notion that every block they traveled brought her closer to… getting naked.

She couldn't. Oh, why couldn't someone invent a time machine, so they could travel to an alternate universe where she could have the figure she once had, the smooth skin, the lean flanks? Where she didn't—

The car swerved to the curb. He jammed it into Park and in an instant had his mouth on hers.

"Wha—" But her question was swallowed up into… glory. Heat. Outrageous hunger.

Just as quickly, he released her. "There. You're thinking too much."

She was miles behind him, scrambling. "You're out of your mind."

A slash of white teeth. "You will be, too, very shortly, if I have any say over it." He began driving again, but shot her a glance. "And I intend to."

She hopped from one thought to another and couldn't settle on any notion of how to feel. What to say.

And the long, sweet pull in her belly was…amazing.

So she let her head fall back on the seat and released a shaky laugh. "Can't you drive any faster?"

"You have no mercy." He punched the accelerator. He gave a chuckle, but it wasn't much steadier. "I like that about you."

Together, they shot through the night.

HE TRIED, he really tried. He'd planned to draw her out of the car and escort her inside, chat a little to relax her as he opened the champagne he'd been chilling. Cristal, the only choice for a diamond of the first water, as Anne was.

But as though they were kids, the second he had her

door open, he was pulling her to her feet and plastering her against the car, racing his mouth over her throat, her face…those astonishing lips of hers.

Then she slid her foot up his leg, and whatever thoughts he'd had were sucked up into a cyclone and scattered here and yon.

Somehow, they made it inside. He was carrying her, that much he knew, but the details of keys and doors were hazy, lost in kisses as much hers as his, in small hands sliding into his hair, over his shoulders.

In the feel of something precious in his arms that he wanted to never let go.

Blindly, he made his way to the destination he had, thank God, preprogrammed into his brain, or heaven knows where they might have ended up. He tore his mouth from hers with just enough presence of mind to say, "Close your eyes."

She looked up at him, those pupils huge and dark and mystified and…filled with the secrets only women knew. Ones men spent their entire lives trying to unlock.

"Please," he asked hoarsely.

Silently, she complied.

He set her on her feet with great reluctance. Cupped her face in his hands. "Stand here for a minute. Don't look, all right?"

She nodded, and he kissed that mouth, pouring all he was into it. Only barely did he manage to tear himself away.

Then he raced around like a madman, lighting candles, snagging the Cristal and a bucket of ice.

Hoping like hell he wasn't making a fool of himself.

But he hadn't wanted their first time to be in a bedroom either had inhabited with someone else, or in a hotel room, either, however luxurious. So he went for her favorite room in his house, and felt pride in having such a spot.

Because he wanted this night to be about pleasure for her. About respite and peace, though maybe not too much peace, he grinned to himself. But a glimpse for her of what the future could be.

Would be, if he had any choice in the matter.

God willing, he would.

Finally, he was done, and he paused only for an instant to look at her, surrounded by flowers but eclipsing them all.

Let me do right by her. Please.

"Okay," he said. "You can look now."

He hadn't been this nervous since he was sixteen.

ANNE SMELLED the flowers before she saw them. Breathed in the rich scent of earth and blossoms, signs of hope and beginnings. Slowly, she lifted her lashes.

"Oh." She sighed at the beauty of it. Moonlight poured through the glass ceiling, leaf-dappled and lovely. Candles glowed, small golden blooms amid a riot of red and orange, white and hot pink.

And in the center of a space he'd cleared, a daybed, a wide one. Plump cushions in rich tones of burgundy and bronze, forest-green and cerulean blue. A silver bucket stood nearby with a bottle inside and two flutes on a small table.

"Oh, William…it's stunning."

He caught her hand, brought it, as he often did, to his lips. "A pale backdrop for your beauty, Anne."

The nerves in his eyes, and the faint tracery of relief, steadied her somehow. She had no idea what to say, except "Thank you."

He let her hand go and walked to the bucket. "Champagne?"

She wanted to ask him to come back. Not to let go. "Yes," she answered. She needed the Dutch courage.

Nonsense. Are you a man or a mouse? An old cartoon character popped into her head.

Well, neither, actually. And she giggled.

William turned, bottle in hand. "What?"

Suddenly, she was laughing. For absolutely no good reason.

As smoothly as he did everything else, he withdrew the cork.

And that set her off again. "Oh, I'm sorry." She fluttered her hands. "Really." And laughed some more. Clapped both hands over her mouth to stop. "I'm…I don't…"

He looked…baffled. And slightly hurt.

Abruptly, she was furious with herself, and that did the trick. "This is ridiculous," she muttered, and marched over to him. Grabbed the flute and downed it like a longshoreman. "There." She slapped it on the table with an abandon that made both of them wince.

"All right." She exhaled. "All right." And began to attack her buttons. "I can do this," she mumbled. "I'm not afraid of you. And if you can't take the sight of it, then just—" She interrupted her rampage to wave him off. "To the devil with you."

"Anne." Suddenly, he was right before her, inches away. Removing her fingers and lowering her hands to her sides, then cradling her face with such tenderness in his own that she knew she would cry. "Beloved," he said. "Trust me."

"I…do. Well, mostly."

His breath moved over her face, a graze of lips here, a soothing of tongue there, until she felt her nerves folding up their nasty little spines and fading away into the darkness.

"Oh." She sighed. "Oh."

He murmured to her as he slid her into a dream. Slipped her last buttons free and let her dress fall with a whisper.

"Oh." Him this time. "You lovely, wicked woman." He scooped her into his arms again, and her head lolled back.

"You like?" she asked of the slip she'd agonized over, with its cunning little peekaboo strips of lace and net.

"Oh, yeah. Let me show you," he said. And proceeded to do exactly that, laying her on silk sheets, removing her shoes with a slide of tongue over her arch that shot her body to a bow.

Then soothing her and teasing her, up her calves to her thighs, and each time she tensed, refusing to let her. Speaking soft, naughty, wonderful suggestions in her ears while his hands drove her nearly past hearing.

"Come here," she begged. "Let me touch you."

"Not yet," was the answer. "This is for you, only you." Slowly and patiently, he retaught her body that it was built for pleasure. That it could rise and soar, leap from peak to peak, until a beg became a moan, then all but a scream.

"William—" She grasped for him. Arched for him. "Not alone. Please. I've been solitary—" Too long. Oh, too long.

Suddenly, he was there, the heat of him. The glorious…weight of him. The shock and wonder of flesh against flesh made her whimper. "Not alone…"

"No." His voice was harsh with strain and demand. "Never again, do you hear me?" He parted her legs, and she bit her lip. Grabbed hold of him and dug in claws.

"Now, William, now."

His arms were so strong as he held himself from her. "Look at me." But his voice was as much plea as command. "You will never again be alone. I'm with you, and I'm staying. Tell me you want that. Want me."

So blue, sky-blue those eyes, but with thunder rumbling in the distance. Demanding notice. Acceptance.

Boiling up from within her were tears and need, longing and so, so much loneliness. "I can't need you. I want you, but I can't…I'm afraid to need you."

"You will." He brushed against her, and she gasped at the feel of him. "You do. And I do, Anne. I need you. We're not accustomed to it, either of us, but that doesn't matter." He slid inside, barely inside, achingly so. "Get used to it, love. Let me in, Anne," and she knew he was speaking of much more than the joining of their bodies. "I'm trying hard to give you time to catch up with loving me, but…catch up," he whispered. "Please."

She'd thought it would be so difficult, but suddenly it was so easy. So…right. "Yes," she said, almost too softly for her own ears. Then again, louder. With her heart, which had thought this, for her, was over.

"Yes."

He closed his eyes. "Thank God." Then opened them, blazing. "I swear I—"

She grabbed his head. Kissed him hard. "Don't swear. Just come with me, William. Please…be with me."

A long, smooth glide, and they were there, together, in a new place. One not entirely unfamiliar but unshared by past loves, one simply…theirs.

Beautifully, perfectly…thank the stars, theirs.

CHAPTER TEN

"MOONLIGHT BECOMES YOU," William quoted an old song as he traced one finger over Anne's hairline. Lifted a strand and kissed it, then tickled her jaw with the end.

She sighed without opening her eyes. "I feel…glorious." She stretched her arms above her head, wiggled her toes. Then looked at him. "Thank you for—" she glanced around the conservatory "—this. It's my favorite part of your home."

"I know."

She cut him a glance. "Think you're pretty smart, don't you?"

He waggled his eyebrows. "I do now."

She laughed. "A regular Lothario, are you? Expert at seduction?"

"No." He sobered completely. "No, Anne. I won't let you be flippant about this. It's too important to me."

"I'm sorry." Her contrition showed.

Before she could go on, he answered the question she hadn't asked. "I've never made love in here before. Ever."

Her eyes widened. "Ever?"

"No." He wasn't going to breach the privacy of his marriage; Isabel deserved better. She might not have been adventurous, but she'd been a good woman and their years together had been happy ones. So he moved on. "And I don't consider seduction a sport."

Remorse was draining away her glow, and he didn't want that. "I've exhausted my supply of adjectives, so I'll repeat myself." He kissed her fingers. "You are amazing." He turned her palm and did the same. "So beautiful I can't stop drinking in the sight of you." He indulged himself in a slow scan of her body under the sheet she'd dragged over herself. "One of these days, you're going to let me look my fill."

"Don't count on it," she said tartly. "But thank you for the candles. They're very forgiving."

"Anne." He counseled himself to patience. "You're welcome. But we will be doing this again, and I will be looking at you. All of you. In every kind of light." He cradled her cheek. "We're neither of us young, but we bring so much more to the table. Once I would have already had you again, now I make up for frequency with, I'd like to think, finesse. A caring for my partner and insights into her needs that a young man doesn't yet understand. Or at least, I hope that's true."

She rolled to her side and propped her head on one hand. "Oh, it is…" She ran her hand over his shoulder, trailed fingers down his chest. "Very true indeed." Her smile was wide and wicked. "I'm sorry. It's impossible not to wish that I could show you how great I used to look. Except, of course, I was married then and would never have—" She lifted one shoulder. "You know."

"I do." He was beyond relieved when she didn't draw

away after bringing up Remy. "What I want you to understand is that I love how you look right now." He grinned. "Especially right now." He nuzzled her throat. Breathed in the scent of her. Felt need waking in him again. And wasn't that just a kick?

He had no idea if he could convince her to stay the night, not yet. He'd simply prolong the pleasure for both of them for a bit. See what transpired. "I mentioned Estelle's cake. You hungry?"

Her eyes widened. "Starving. But I never eat late at night."

He rose from the bed and slipped on his trousers, already wishing they could remain there forever. "The night is young, my dear. Stay where you are. I'll be right back."

Her eyes were luminous. "I'm not sure I can move, anyway," she said in a low, silky tone.

He stopped where he was. "You kill me. Just absolutely destroy me."

She blushed prettily. "Hurry back."

Oh, he would. He definitely would. Except. "I don't want to leave you." He let all pretense of flirting drop and did something that was uncharacteristic of him. Allowed exactly what he felt to shine through, vulnerable though it made him.

She stared at him in silence, her own expression revealing her confusion. And, he thought, a sizable amount of longing.

"Come with me." He held out a hand.

She sat up, clutching the sheet, glancing around her.

He picked up his shirt, understanding the problem. "Here. Take this for now, and I'll find you a robe." Then he forced himself to turn his back. He'd get her past this reticence, by God. Make her see herself through his eyes. *One step at a time*, he reminded himself. *She's in your house. Your bed, if not the permanent one upstairs.*

Her hand slipped into his, and he squeezed it. Drew her close.

When her arms stole round his waist, he bent his head to hers.

And savored.

SHE STROLLED AROUND his kitchen barefoot, chatting with him while he made coffee, trailing the hem of his much-too-large navy robe like the train of a ball gown. Every once in a while, she'd catch it up or flick it aside, and he'd be treated to a flash of leg. The sleeves were rolled up three times and still nearly covered her hands, which she used so gracefully to emphasize a point. To touch his granite counters or graze over a canister. Brush across the leaves of the herbs Estelle kept in a sunny window.

Until he thought he'd do anything to have them on him again.

She was a sprite with a queen's bearing. A small woman whose heart and courage were several times her size. As was her stubbornness.

He was crazy about her.

Wanted—no, needed—to protect her.

And hoped like hell she'd believe that when she knew what he'd done.

Because he wasn't losing her.

"That's quite a frown."

He blinked. "Huh? Oh—nothing. Just, uh, thinking about whether we have ice cream to go with the cake."

Her expression said she wasn't buying that, but she let it pass. "I have no business eating this. My doctor would, you'll excuse the pun, have a heart attack at the thought." She grinned.

The topic drained everything else from his head. "What was I thinking?" He retracted the plate he'd been about to offer. "You'll have to teach me what you can and can't have. Your health is too important—"

"Gimme," she said. Snagged the plate right out of his hand. Laughed as he refused to let go. "William, it was a joke."

"Your welfare is no laughing matter to me, Anne. I want you around for a long time to come."

"Thank you. I want that, too. I—it was a very sobering experience, one I don't take lightly. I'm careful, but I'm not going to live the rest of my life in fear. I take the steps that are required, but even my doctor agrees that flexibility is important. That you can do a better job of a strict regimen if you allow yourself some lapses, as long as they're not frequent. So I exercise and I eat exactly what I should most of the time—and then I sin here and there."

"How recently was your last occasion of sin?"

"Don't even go there." She set the cake down. Took his hands. "William, I'm trying to let you into my life, even though I don't begin to know what to do with you.

But I don't need a mother or a nanny or a keeper, *comprends?* Maybe my business isn't thriving right now, but what success I've had is because I've been very disciplined. I still am."

"I'm sorry. I wasn't trying—"

"Yes, you were." But she softened her tone. "You care about me, and that means more than I can say, even if I can't quite put you in a slot, and that troubles me."

He frowned. "I don't fit in slots."

She laughed. "You're telling me." She shook her head. Cut a sideways glance at him. "You take up a lot of room, you know that? Not just physically, either."

"Get used to it. I intend to take up more."

"Maybe," she warned. "I haven't decided that yet."

But he could see past her bravado. "You have. You just don't like it. I'm onto you, Anne Marchand." He tugged at the fingers she had shoved into the pockets of his robe. Gripped them. "I never thought I'd pity Remy, but I doubt that man ever had the final say—or if he did, it was only because you'd had your fill of arguing." He laughed at her scowl. Nipped at her knuckles. "Don't pout."

"I never pout." Her tone was frosty.

He reeled her in. "I love your independence nearly as much as I despair of it. I believe I've said before that you're a challenge."

Her resistance was only token. "You pirates are all alike. You'd crack up under a routine. That's why you and I would never suit."

He shouted his laughter. "Because you're such a stick in the mud? A devotee of the mundane?"

She mock-punched his shoulder. "You're spoiled. You've never met an obstacle you couldn't conquer. You're too used to getting your way."

"Well, you've certainly seen to that, haven't you?" He kissed her and told himself it wasn't to shut her up.

What was between them flared white-hot again.

She broke away. "Stick in the mud, huh?"

"I didn't say—"

She deepened the kiss. Backed him against the counter. "You might think you're getting your way this time, too, but I just want to be sure you know that you're only getting lucky."

He laughed. "Whatever you want to believe."

She pulled his head back down.

"Okay, uncle," he murmured in the brief space of a stolen breath. "I'm spoiled, I'm a pirate, I'm…anything else I need to confess? Oh, yes. Lucky."

She started to answer, but he dove right back in. "Lucky as hell." He snatched her up and headed back for their love nest.

The cake would have to wait.

THEY WERE GETTING crumbs in the bed, Anne thought as they sat facing, feeding each other with their fingers.

Sweet stars above, she felt wonderful. Whole body singing, the tune a bawdy one, accompanied by strings…occasionally breaking out into the "Hallelujah Chorus."

She giggled. "I feel fantastic."

He grinned. "You are." He slid one thumb over her cheek and retrieved frosting. Licked it off. Slowly.

Taunting her. Daring.

Her breath seized. "You can't possibly."

One eyebrow arched. "You sure?" Then he smiled. "Probably not, but then, you seem to have a unique effect on me. I feel like a kid again."

"You're pretty yummy yourself, Mr. Armstrong."

"Yummy." Color stained his cheeks and delighted her. "I don't recall that anyone's ever used that word for me before."

Mon Dieu, the man upended her whole world. She had no business having any fun at all, not when everything she'd worked almost forty years for was in peril.

But, oh, how tired she was, sometimes, of being so strong. Yes, she was strong, always had been. Always would be. But was it so wrong to enjoy being with William? Experiencing the sheer relief of having someone to share her burdens? Feeling so…young, as if her cares didn't have to occupy her every waking minute?

"Penny for your thoughts," he said.

She jolted back into the moment. "What if they're worth more?" she teased.

"Then I'll pay it."

"Might be pricey."

He shrugged. "So be it."

Eerie how closely he tracked her thoughts. But comforting, too. She sighed. "William, I can't afford to be distracted right now."

"I'd prefer to be an asset." He set aside the plate. "Seriously, Anne. Isn't there some way I can help you?"

"You do, more than you realize." At his huff of impatience, she sat up on her knees. "I'm not kidding. I know you're there, ready and waiting. I don't expect you to understand why I have to do this myself, but it means everything to me that you don't shove your way in and take over." A pained expression crossed his face, and she wanted to lighten it. "Not that I'd let you." A quick grin, but her heart wasn't in it. "I promise you that if things get too bad, I'll ask for help."

His gloom didn't lighten. "Don't wait that long. It makes no sense to delay when there are options."

"Maybe not," she said. "Perhaps I was doomed from the beginning." Doubts, never far from the surface, crept in. "But if I can't make it on my own, with my girls' help, then maybe it's just as well. Remy's dream—my dream, too—wasn't to be swallowed up by some chain. What we created was unique. If it can't continue as it was, then maybe it's best to let it go. Move on." She stared into the distance. Then, with a concerted effort, she shook off her sorrow. "But we're not there yet. We have this new offer to consider. I don't want to take it, but whoever it is seems reasonable, thank goodness.

"We have a little breathing room, and we're now booked solid through Mardi Gras. If we have no other catastrophes, we just might manage our way through this. And my girls have hatched some exciting new ideas that could be our future."

Watching her pull herself, once again, from despair was a double-edged sword for William. He found himself well and truly caught now, trapped by his own arrogance. If he withdrew his offer, Anne lost a source of comfort, yet if she found out the offer was his, not only would she not accept it, but her confidence would likely suffer. Along with any trust he'd built up with her.

He found himself, for once in his life, unwilling to gamble any more than he already had. What was between them was too new, too fragile. He couldn't take any more risks or he might lose her. Maybe he'd been hasty in making the offer through Jud, but that was done. He would have to live with it. Be wary and light on his feet to maneuver through this minefield created because he'd gone and fallen in love with her.

He'd had his conversations with their mutual suppliers. The better terms she would get would help the Hotel Marchand's bottom line, but the effect would take time. He had investigators looking into the series of mishaps that had befallen the hotel because he, too, didn't hold much stock in simple bad luck. The Corbins, the brothers who'd made the original offer, were his prime suspects, but they were cagey bastards. Scuttlebutt in the industry had them connected to operations in Thailand that were highly dubious. What they wanted with the Hotel Marchand, he couldn't guess, but he was pressing his men hard to come up with answers.

The mole he'd placed inside the hotel, though, was having difficulties. Like a turtle, the Hotel Marchand had pulled into its shell. Everyone was more guarded lately, so his mole hadn't yet unearthed any evidence that the hotel's recent problems were an inside job.

But he was almost certain that someone in Anne's hotel was at fault. That person needed to be rooted out and questioned for possible links to the Corbins. It was an idea that increasingly made sense to William, that undermining the hotel's reputation was the quickest way to lower its value and make it a prime plum for the picking.

"And so I decided to paint myself red and march through the Quarter naked."

William snapped to attention. "What? What are you saying?"

"Gotcha," she said. "Where did you go?"

"Sorry." He seized on teasing. "Plotting how to move you upstairs. That bed is bigger."

But he'd alerted her, damn it.

"What time is it?" She glanced around. "Oh, dear. It must be very late. I have to go."

He grasped her shoulder. "Stay. Sleep with me, Anne. I'd like that."

"Oh, William." She sighed. "I would, too, I think."

"Then it's simple."

She kept her eyes steady on him, and her answer was evident. "There's nothing simple about you. Or…this. Whatever it is."

He cautioned himself not to push. Sometimes you lost what you wanted most by gripping it too tightly.

"I'll take you home," he said. "But don't expect me to like it." He summoned a smile.

Her answering one was filled with relief. "If it helps

you, I don't care for it much, either." She rose and gathered her clothes. "I'll just go and change."

He watched her progress through the conservatory. Took heart from how her fingers trailed over a blossom here, how she paused to sniff there.

I'll have you back here, he promised himself as much as her. *Permanently, if I have any say about it.*

And because he was worried that he wouldn't, he spoke before she reached the door. "Anne."

She turned, and the yearning in her face heartened him.

"Love is what this is. Remember it."

She gnawed at her lip for a second. He could almost see the argument rising.

But instead, she blew him a kiss.

He was still grinning long after she was out of his sight.

"SHE'S BACK at the hotel," the man reported. "She and Armstrong look pretty cozy— Whoa!"

"What?" Mike Blount snapped into his phone. "What's going on?"

"She's a grandma, for chrissake. They're wrapped around each other like—" The man chuckled over the line. "Gotta give Armstrong credit. Old dude's got some moves."

"Shut up," Blount ordered. "You're not there for a peep show. Is he staying the night?"

"Sorry." A pause. "Doubt it. He's got his car parked on the street. You don't leave a Jag out like that."

"Follow him."

"Him? Not her?"

"Just do as you're told."

"Yes, sir. If he goes home, then what?"

"Stay with him."

"What about her?"

"I'm switching coverage. I want everyone fresh. No missed details. Everything will speed up soon."

Mike Blount clicked off. Pondered the idiots who posed his biggest trial. This punk was an irritant, but he had a sharp eye.

The Corbins were beginning to be more than a pain in the ass, but he didn't have time to replace them. The deal was getting complicated. Armstrong was one wily bastard. They'd never had dealings, but word got around. Unfortunately, he was also strictly aboveboard. No place to find leverage, as far as Blount's sources could tell.

Could be he was playing the Marchand woman. A smart idea, at that. His background made him suitable for a woman with her pedigree.

But whatever his motivation, his interference couldn't be allowed. Timing was too critical, and this second offer threw a wrench into the works.

Damn good thing he'd been keeping surveillance on everyone surrounding the Marchands, including Armstrong. His tail had seen Armstrong meet with an attorney, Jud Lawson, not his usual firm. Blount had pulled that thread and found Armstrong engaged in some covert activities of his own.

Too bad for Armstrong that his mole inside the hotel had a weakness for the ponies.

Mike Blount smiled, cold as a shark.

William Armstrong was smart and powerful.

But so was he.

LUC'S PHONE RANG in the wee hours. He looked at the display and groaned. Clicked it on. "Yeah. What?"

"William Armstrong has made an offer on the hotel."

"Are you kidding?" His sluggish brain snapped to alert. Armstrong had picked up Anne for a date earlier. Brought lilacs with him. What was he—

"A better one, from what I hear."

Then you're screwed, aren't you? Luc couldn't help but smile. "But you're not certain, right?"

"That's where you come in. You have to find out the terms."

"That's not in my area. It would make no sense for me to know about it, much less expect anyone to tell me the details."

"I don't give a damn what makes sense!" Richard Corbin screamed. "They're screwing up our deal, and there's no time. We can't lose our position. Find out what we're up against, or—"

Luc was heartily sick of the Corbin brothers. "Or what?"

"You don't want to know, trust me. Pray you never find out what happens if you let this go down the tubes. I don't care what you have to do. Break into Charlotte Marchand's office or knock her old lady upside the head and beat it out of her—I don't care, do you hear me? Get me that answer—now."

"It's risky. I can't just go in there and—"

"I told Dan you were gutless. You're down to your last chance, you hear me? If you can't get this information fast, then we don't need you. And what we don't need, we ditch. Got it?"

The connection was severed with a decisive click.

Oh, he got it all right. The day the Corbins were out of his life couldn't come too soon. Break into Charlotte's office? The guy was a head case.

But a more violent one than Luc had ever imagined. He had to buy time.

And he needed answers. A new offer threw a big unknown into an ever more complicated chess game.

He rose from his bed and paced as he tried to reformulate the board.

CHAPTER ELEVEN

IT WAS WRONG to be having so much fun in the midst of such worry, Anne thought as she rose too late for her swim.

But, oh my, this was delicious. William wasn't the only one who felt like a kid again, all breathless and eager the way she remembered being on summer mornings, when a whole day spread before her, hours and hours bright with possibilities. Adventures to share with her friends or—

Her mood dipped. With Pierre. Her beloved younger brother, so long gone.

So much missed. She crossed to the secretary in the corner and withdrew a favorite photo of the two of them, taken when he was about eight and she, twelve. "Oh, *mon frère*," she said. "Where are you?"

There was a knock on her door. She frowned. Who, at this hour?

A peep into the hallway had her shaking her head. Still, she opened the door. "What are you doing here?"

"Taking you to breakfast," William said. "I missed you." From behind his back, he withdrew more flowers. Daisies this time, bright as the morning.

She clutched them to her, ridiculously pleased. "You just saw me."

Again, the eyebrows. "I did. I'm ready to see more."

She couldn't help laughing. "Have you ever heard the phrase, 'Absence makes the heart grow fonder'?"

He gathered her close. Nipped at her bottom lip. "It's been hours. Days."

"You are insane." But she sank into the kiss. "Mmm…" She licked the taste of it from her lips.

His eyes darkened. He began to back her toward her bedroom.

"Stop." She plastered a hand to his chest. "Don't you have business to conduct?"

He waltzed her in a circle, ever closer to the bed. "So perceptive of you to notice. Though, strictly speaking, not the same sort of business I care to share with my associates."

He had her off her feet then, swinging her in dizzying arcs.

She clutched him tightly. And let herself revel, just for a minute, in an adventure she would never have dreamed of as a girl.

Next thing she knew, she was flat on her back on her mattress, and her robe was parted. William delivered a series of devastating kisses to the flesh revealed, an expanse that seemed to increase with each passing second.

It was daylight, if only weak morning sun. She should be paralyzed by worry.

Instead, she was shivering with delight. Moaning in a most unladylike manner. "William, I—"

Whatever she might have said, had she been able to

think straight, dissolved under the assault of his mouth. His hands. Oh, those hands, they made her absolutely…hot.

She had to smile. Who would have imagined? Her daughters would be scandalized. They were right here in the hotel—or would be—very soon.

She tried to summon the will to stop William. Send him away.

Then he shot a jolt right through her veins that scrambled the last vestige of her logic.

Think…later.

William…now.

She gave herself up to the ministrations of a man who did indeed understand everything about…finesse.

"YOUR SHIRT IS WRINKLED," Anne said, some time later, following him into the living room as he knotted his tie.

"I have an extra at my office." But he thought he might keep this one for a trophy. Her scent clung to it.

He was hopeless. What's worse, he didn't much care. If there were any way to cancel his next meeting, he'd scoop her up and spirit her away. He had a cabin in Montana, where it was still winter. Long, cold nights in front of a fire.

"Get that look off your face," she said.

"What look?"

Her gaze narrowed. "That…panther sizing up prey expression."

"Guilty as charged." He grinned. "But you'd like it, I promise you that."

Her cheeks went pink. Charmed the hell out of him. "I'm sure I would, more's the pity. But you have an empire to run, and I have a hotel in trouble. I've been unconscionably negligent."

"You had dinner. You have to eat."

"We also had breakfast." She all but wrung her hands. "And…you know. Sex."

His amusement fled. "It was more than sex. Don't deny it."

"No." Her voice was very quiet. "I won't. And maybe someday, when this is all over—if it ever is—I'll figure out what to do about it. About you."

He reached for her.

"Keep your hands to yourself. They should be classified as lethal weapons." She was striving to tease, but he heard the strain.

"I refuse," he said, as he reeled her in, keeping his gaze locked on hers. "But I will let you get to work, after this one thing."

"What thing?" Suspicion colored her tone.

"Just this." He throttled back on the gnawing need he had for her and set himself to soothe, wrapping her in his arms and simply holding her. "Not so bad, is it?"

She sighed and settled. "Not bad at all."

"I love you," he murmured. "I wish that didn't trouble you."

Her arms tightened. "Maybe it won't much longer."

He would have to be content with that progress, limited as it felt. "I can only live in hope," he said dryly.

Her faint chuckle—and the snuggle that accompanied it—was his reward.

After a few precious moments, he released her, if grudgingly. Slipped on his suit jacket, reached for his keys on the entry table. Saw the photo. "What's this?" He answered his own question. "You and…your brother?" He turned to her. "Still can't find him?"

She shook her head. "I'm sorry to say that I haven't had a chance to look for a new investigator after the previous one failed to turn up anything useful."

This he could do for her. "Let me. I have a firm that's top-notch."

"You don't have to—"

"Please, Anne." He fought to keep the annoyance from his voice and only partially succeeded. "I want to help. For God's sake, at least let me do this."

He saw the struggle within her. Waited for the refusal.

But she surprised him. "Thank you. I'd appreciate it."

He swooped in, planted a quick kiss. "That wasn't so hard, now was it?"

She let out a breath. "Yes." She gifted him with a smile. "But maybe with practice, I'll get better at it."

"You're going to catch up, aren't you?" he said quietly, one hand on the knob.

She met his gaze full-on. "Probably, yes."

Cheered, he stole one more kiss. "That's my girl. Pick you up at seven."

And was out the door before she could argue.

He heard her laughter ring behind him as he strode down the hall.

LUC WAS IN Charlotte's office when they heard Anne outside with Charlotte's assistant Julie.

"She sounds happy," he remarked.

"She does." Charlotte smiled.

"The date must have gone well last night," he said.

"What date?" Charlotte's eyes narrowed. "Don't tell me. William Armstrong."

Luc thought about Anne's voice on the phone last night. How she'd told him William could have full access from now on.

Then he remembered Corbin's call.

"Yes." His heart sank. When she found out…

Charlotte's mouth pursed, but whatever she'd meant to say was lost to Anne's entrance.

"*Doucette,* I—oh, Luc, I'm sorry. Julie didn't say there was a meeting." Her smile was blinding. "But then, I didn't give her much chance."

"We're done here," Charlotte responded.

Luc wasn't, but he'd managed all the surreptitious examination of the papers on her desk he could while carrying on a coherent conversation about a tour group set to arrive tomorrow.

Anne's expression turned serious. "Is anything wrong? Anything else…happen?"

At the loss of her joy, Luc experienced his strongest pang of regret to date. He'd done this to her. To them. His grandmother deserved any pain that could be meted out, but his aunt and his cousins had done nothing. The more time he spent around them, the more certain he was that he and his mother would have been welcomed by this part of the Robichaux clan.

And now, the man who'd made her so happy was double-dealing her. He had to warn her, but how did he explain that he knew? If he blew his cover, he was useless to them.

"No, nothing," he hastened to add. "Just last-minute details on the Sun West group."

When her face cleared, it was a gift he hadn't earned. "We'll do fine." She patted his arm. "Have we told you lately, Luc, how lucky we are to have you? Mrs. Davis caught me yesterday after her massage. The woman couldn't say enough about you."

Lower than a snake's belly, he felt. "She found me again last night."

"Oh, yes. William told me about it. Said our future bookings should reflect her satisfaction."

"Did you have a good time, I hope?"

Color rushed to not only Anne's cheeks but her entire face, her throat. "Um, yes. It was…lovely. Good food."

He and Charlotte exchanged glances. Charlotte's brows snapped together. The most protective of Anne's daughters, she was clearly unhappy.

The moment was awkward. He decided on rescue. "So what did you have to eat?"

A relieved Anne launched into a description of the restaurant, its decor and the dishes they'd sampled. She seemed ready to move to a comparison with their own menu.

"Luc has to go, *Mère*," Charlotte interrupted. Her glance at him was pure dismissal.

He had the urge to remain to protect Anne from her daughter's disapproval. But Charlotte was the boss. "I do, I'm sorry to say. Perhaps you could drop by later to chat more?"

"Oh. Well, I—" Anne Marchand, always composed, was clearly discombobulated. It endeared her to him more than ever.

"You're busy, too, of course." He let her off the hook. "I'm glad you had a good time. It's much-deserved."

"Why, thank you."

"That will be all, Luc." Charlotte's tone was nearly as crisp as the glare she shot at him.

"Good day, ladies." If he hadn't heard about Armstrong's offer, he'd be grinning. *You go, Aunt Anne*.

Instead, his mind was in an uproar, trying to sort out a viable solution. He understood so little about the dynamics of a close family like this. There'd only been his mother and himself for most of his life. She'd loved him, but she'd been so beaten down by the struggles and consumed by her bitterness over Pierre's betrayal and his family's disdain that he'd never experienced anything like what the Marchands shared, that powerful family tie that no amount of disagreement could unravel. That sense of always having someone at your back. A rock-solid understanding of who you were and where you belonged.

And he'd bought into the assumption of Anne's and his grandmother's guilt without questioning. He'd been bent on avenging wrongs against his father that now appeared to be only due to his grandmother's unforgiving nature.

He could have belonged to this family under different circumstances.

Now he never would.

He was so intent on his thoughts that he knocked into a passing maintenance man. "Excuse me."

The man, built like a fireplug, moved past. "No problem."

Luc looked back. Frowned. A new employee he hadn't met—

I'm sending in a team. They have a lot of skills besides arson. Just then, the man rounded a corner, and Luc realized what he should have seen before. The man was wearing street shoes—shiny shoes, not work boots—with a hotel uniform.

He stood, frozen. If he stopped the man, the Corbins would hear, all too soon, and he'd be out of the loop, powerless to protect Anne or her daughters.

But if he didn't, there'd be a fire, sometime soon. Without notice.

Or worse.

He could follow the guy discreetly, but he was no spy.

A mirthless laugh erupted. Of course he was. Just not a very good one. An idiot who'd gotten himself tangled up with some very bad people. And if the man he'd just seen caught him following, the result would be the same. The Corbins would cut him out of the picture.

Pray you never find out what happens if you let this go down the tubes. Richard's threat.

He had to figure a way out. In the meantime, he needed to warn the Marchands about Armstrong's offer. But how?

Then a solution hit him. An anonymous note to Charlotte would tip her off. Each employee had a mailbox, and he had easy access to accomplish that. Maybe Anne knew who was behind the offer, but he had no way to ask that question, as it was clearly not his business. Maybe she was fine with it.

But if not, Charlotte was relentless. She would track down the details and guard her mother, to boot.

And he would stall for time with the Corbins. In nine days, it would be Mardi Gras, and this would all be over.

Nine days for him to work out some way to make the Corbins change their minds.

And leave the Hotel Marchand alone.

CHAPTER TWELVE

LATE IN THE AFTERNOON, Charlotte made her way back to her office, sorting through the mail she'd picked up from her in-house mailbox.

She frowned at the plain white envelope with her name typed on the front, and curiosity had her opening it first. Rapidly, she scanned the unsigned note inside.

And sank into her chair. Stared.

WILLIAM ARMSTRONG = SECOND OFFER???

No. Oh, dear heaven, no—

That bastard. Smooth-talking, slick sonofa—

The image of her mother this morning flashed through her mind. She'd been so happy, her feet barely touching the ground.

Blushing, for heaven's sake, like a girl.

Why would he do this to Mama?

Charlotte shoved to her feet. Craved to throw something. If she were a man, she'd—

Hold it, her better sense prevailed. *Don't go off half-cocked. You have no idea who sent this. Be sure before you—*

She sagged. She would have to tell her mother. Oh, mercy, how could she ever break news like this?

Then a notion hit her, a means to confirm this quickly. She picked up the phone and dialed. Jud Lawson had submitted the second offer as trustee. She tapped her toes while she waded through voice mail.

Why didn't anyone have a live person answering phones anymore?

Finally, she reached the option to dial his extension. "Jud Lawson's office."

Not him. She ground her teeth at yet one more delay.

Wait. Maybe if she—

"This is Judith Armstrong, calling for my father about the offer on the Hotel Marchand. You might be able to help me with a quick question."

"I'd be happy to, but the file is in Mr. Lawson's office."

Bingo. But she couldn't feel glad.

"Is he available?"

"He is, Ms. Armstrong. Let me get him."

She took in a deep breath. Then another. Wondered if she could bear to see this through.

"Ms. Armstrong, I'm surprised to hear from you."

You're about to be more surprised. "This is Charlotte Marchand. Is William Armstrong behind the offer you submitted?" She had to be certain.

His sharp intake of breath told her all she needed to know. He recovered quickly, but not quickly enough. "That's privileged information, as I'm sure you're aware."

"Oh, I am." She counseled herself to slow down. They might need that offer.

The hell they would. She'd sell this hotel over her dead body. She'd slaved and sweated for months now with barely a day off, trying to step into her mother's very formidable shoes, at first mostly because it was a family enterprise.

Then because the hotel was hers. She loved this place, every stone, every nook, every cranny. The dread that they were going to lose it was a constant chill in her bones. If they did, her mother would forgive her, she knew that.

But she would not forgive herself.

"You may not choose to confirm the identity of the buyer, but you can certainly relay an answer for me, can't you, Mr. Lawson?" She forced her voice to sweetness and nearly gagged.

"I suppose."

"Well, you tell William Armstrong—I mean, your client, that hell will freeze over before I sell to him."

"My client's identity will remain anonymous until he or she chooses to reveal it. That said, I believe your mother is the only person who can exercise the option to sell."

"That's the other part of this. You inform him that he'd better stay away from my mother, or—" Barely, barely, she reined herself in. Her father's temper had been legendary, and she was a chip off the old block.

"I wouldn't make threats, Ms. Marchand. This is a simple, straightforward business transaction. Your conduct is unprofessional."

She clenched her jaw. Counted to ten.

"My conduct—" She swallowed hard, tamped down the bitter words rushing to be said. "Just pass along my message, Mr. Lawson."

She didn't wait for his response before she slammed down the phone.

"Charlotte, you have that appointment—" Her assistant halted in the doorway. "What's wrong?"

"Where's my mother?"

"I'll check. Is she okay?"

She won't be.

Oh, for someone to take this off her shoulders, Charlotte begged, this one last thing that felt as though it would send her to her knees.

She would have to break her mother's heart.

Before *he* succeeded in stealing her hotel.

Sweet-talking, lying creep. She'd never trusted him. Why hadn't she kept after her mother, urging her to be more cautious?

"Charlotte?"

"She'll be fine," Charlotte reassured Julie. And hoped she was right. "Please see if you can locate her, but don't tell her I'm looking."

"You got it." Julie left.

Charlotte paced. *Oh, Papa, if only you were here, none of this would have happened.*

She'd never missed her father more.

JUDITH ARMSTRONG stepped off the plane from Dallas, a woman with a mission. She'd done as her father asked, and he would be pleased with what she'd accomplished. She'd been up late last night, preparing a presentation detailing her suggestions for improving profits.

But when she'd finished, she'd been unable to sleep.

A new twist on the Hotel Marchand offer had come to her, and she'd called Glen Schaefer at home to bounce it off him. Not a massive change, but a new angle to make the whole purchase go much more smoothly and remove the last of the objections Anne Marchand might have. Except for the price, of course. But Judith's job was to protect Regency's interests, not theirs.

Armed with that knowledge and a go-ahead from Glen, she would phone and ask for a meeting with Charlotte Marchand. Ostensibly, she was one hotelier making contact with a contemporary. Charlotte was reputed to possess a keen intellect, but so did Judith. It was that incisive mind that had ferreted out her husband's infidelity when he'd been sure he was so much smarter.

Her self-confidence had taken a big slap, and she'd been in a funk for months, but she was hitting her stride now. She was good at this; Glen knew it, and so did her father. She was more a chip off the old block than she'd thought.

Her father had gotten rich by not being afraid to gamble while still being cagey and, when it suited him, circumspect.

She was ready to show him that she could do the same.

She dialed the Hotel Marchand main number. She would meet with Charlotte and manage to feel her out, ever so discreetly, about any desire Charlotte might have to convince her mother to sell or what would be required for an offer to succeed. She would also discover whether Charlotte knew that their parents were…involved. And if that were as distasteful to her as it was to Judith.

The undertaking would require immense skill and delicacy. The Judith so whipped by her failure at marriage wouldn't have believed herself capable of it. Even now, she felt more butterflies than she'd like.

But she was beginning to see that breeding came through. Her father was energized by a gamble, and she felt the buzz of this one in her own blood.

You can do this, she repeated to herself like a mantra. *And Daddy will be so proud.*

"YOUR MOTHER IS ON-SITE," Julie said. "In the courtyard, doing her hostess thing and charming the daylights out of the guests, as always." She grinned. "Wasn't she cute this morning? I swear her feet barely touched the ground. A man, right?"

Charlotte rubbed her forehead. "Yeah. But not just any man. William Armstrong."

"Oh. From The Regency?"

Charlotte nodded.

"He's really rich. And hot, for an older guy."

"He's slime," Charlotte snapped.

"Whoa. He's taking advantage of our Anne?"

Charlotte paused for a second, wishing she could recall her outburst. Then sighed. Julie had proven herself discreet over and over.

And Charlotte could use someone to bounce this off, since her usual sounding board—her mother—was the topic. "He's behind the second offer on the hotel."

Julie's eyes went wide. "No way." Her brows snapped together. "Oh, that's low. That snake." Then she cocked her head. "But it's a good one. Better than the first. Why would he do that?"

This was why Julie was worth her weight in gold. "Because he's seduced Mama into sharing details of the first one, so he knew what to beat?"

"She wouldn't," Julie said. "Unless she—"

"Trusted him," Charlotte finished.

"Oh, no. He really is a jerk."

"He didn't get that rich by being soft." Charlotte thought back. "He and my father had some feud when they were younger. This isn't the first time he's tried to buy the hotel."

"So that's why there's a trustee. So you wouldn't hold the past against him."

Hearing her own thoughts reflected back wasn't comforting. "And to keep Mama from clamming up."

"You have to tell her." Julie looked sad. "She's going to be—"

"Devastated. Yeah." Charlotte's head drooped. She stared at her desktop. "I don't know how to break it to her. And I'd give nearly anything not to have to."

"You should gather your sisters first."

"You know me too well."

"I'll call them." Julie headed for the door. "Oh. I nearly forgot why I came in here. Oh, man…"

"What is it?"

Julie waved a phone message slip. "Guess who wants to drop by to meet you?"

"No idea."

"Judith Armstrong."

Charlotte did a double take. "No way. When?"

"She said at your convenience, but she could drop by on her way back to the office if you could spare a few minutes. She was at the airport."

Charlotte sank back in her chair. "What could she want?" She shook her head. "We're not completely unknown to each other. We went to the same school, though she's younger. We didn't hang around, but she lived close to *Grand-mère*. Her father still does." At the thought of William Armstrong, she frowned again. "How does this fit in?"

"Beats me," Julie said. "So what do I tell her?"

Charlotte's smile was slow and not altogether nice. "Oh, by all means, tell her to drop by. I'll give her a minute."

"And your sisters?"

"Hold off on that until I sort out what in the devil game the Armstrongs are playing."

"You got it."

JUDITH HAD INDEED been in transit from the airport and willing to detour. She no doubt believed that she'd been discreet in the way she'd slipped those probes, so smooth and slick, into a hi-how-are-you, we're-in-the-same-business, just-wanted-to-get-to-know-you excuse for a meeting.

They'd even managed to slide into the territory of common friends, while Charlotte wondered if she'd ever get to the point.

But after Judith had begun her hotel chitchat, she'd become more obvious.

And less so. Because what she seemed to be doing was feeling Charlotte out on what it would take to buy the Hotel Marchand. As if an offer wasn't already in place.

What were they doing? Father and daughter, tag-teaming the Marchands? Judith seemed inordinately interested in determining Charlotte's requirements for giving her blessing to the enterprise.

Finally, Charlotte lost it. "Cut to the chase," she said to Judith. "You've already covered that ground."

"What?" Judith's expression appeared honestly bewildered. "I don't know what you mean."

"The offer your father has submitted. We haven't responded, so why are you fine-tuning now?"

"My…father," Judith said. And all the air seemed to leak out of her.

"So, what, you and he split forces? He seduces my mother and you pump me for information?"

Judith went very pale. "Seduced your mother?"

"Don't tell me you didn't know. He's got her walking around, lit up like a Christmas tree." Charlotte let her contempt drip through every word.

"You're not happy about them, either."

"About him being such a lowlife and so desperate to top my father that he would stoop to breaking the heart of the best woman I've ever met? No, I'm not happy. He's as much a bastard as I feared."

"He's a good man—" The protest was automatic. "He wouldn't do that."

"He already has."

Judith rose, appearing thoroughly shattered. "I can't— He never said a word—" She pressed her lips together. "I have to go. To talk to him. Find out what's going on." She made her way to the door without saying goodbye.

"Wait." Charlotte rounded the desk. "When you see him, let him know that I'm telling my mother now. I'm worried about what it's going to do to her, but she has to be warned. Has to see him for what he really is."

"I understand." Judith's voice was dull.

"Tell him this, as well. If he sets one foot on Hotel Marchand property or tries to contact my mother in any manner, I will have him arrested for stalking, at a minimum. Fraud or anything else I can manage."

"That's absurd."

"Charges might not stick, but his reputation will take a hit. A guy like him has an ego. I'm going to punch a hole in it. I wish I could punch his face."

"He's my father." Judith looked very young suddenly. "He's all I have."

"She's my mother," Charlotte responded fiercely. "I'll do whatever it takes to protect her." Desperately, she mused over options and wondered if her mother could be dissuaded by anything less than the truth.

And knew she wouldn't.

Judith left without responding.

Charlotte sat for a moment with her head in her hands.

Then she reached for the phone to call her sisters.

Mama would need all of them.

ANNE HUMMED SOFTLY as she made her way through the courtyard. Then laughed at herself. She'd been like this all day, barely able to keep her joy from bubbling over. Yes, it was all right to be happy—

It is, Remy, isn't it? He's not you. He could never replace you—

Ma belle, she could almost hear him say. *I am one of a kind.* He would be amused. Well, no, actually, he'd have already raged over to William, fists at the ready, if he were alive. He'd been a very jealous husband.

For a second, her delight dimmed. Then she reminded herself that Remy was not alive. And that he'd been clear that he would never want her alone and without love.

He does love me, Remy. That's what he says, and how he acts, at least. And I think I believe him.

But Remy didn't answer, of course. It was up to her to take the next step in the journey William was clearly bent on making with her. *You're going to catch up, aren't you?*

She'd told him yes. And meant it.

Mostly. It was only that she'd never envisioned loving again. That was the explanation for the tiny hesitation that still dogged her. This was all so new…so unexpected. And she'd left impulsiveness behind when she'd left girlhood.

She smiled, thinking of the way she'd backed William against the counter. Surprising him.

Maybe she hadn't forgotten spontaneity altogether. She considered going shopping for a new outfit for their date tonight, but there wasn't really time. As a matter of fact, she'd better move along.

"Mrs. Marchand."

She turned at the sound of the voice. "Hi, Julie. Isn't it past time for you to get off work? Mac's surely waiting for you."

Mac Jensen was head of his own security business but he'd been working for the Hotel Marchand for the past several months. He'd taken the job to keep an eye on Julie, and in the end, the two of them had fallen in love. Anne would miss Mac, who was winding up his work at the hotel, but at least they'd stay in touch through Julie.

Julie seemed flustered. "He will be, but he understands my job. He doesn't exactly keep office hours himself."

"No, I imagine he doesn't. I'm grateful that we still have him, but I don't want either of you working too hard."

"It's that season," Julie said.

"So true. After Mardi Gras, we'll all breathe easier. So what's on your mind?"

"Charlotte asked me to find you. She'd like to meet you in your quarters, if that's all right."

"Is she okay? Has something happened?"

Julie seemed very uneasy. "She just…needs to talk with you."

Anne thought about her daughter's tears of the previous afternoon. The pressure she was under. "Of course." She didn't have much time to get ready for her date, but if her daughter needed her, William would understand, she was certain. They could delay their dinner. Or postpone if needed. "I'll head there right now."

"Thank you. I could walk with you."

Anne shot her a sideways glance. "That's very sweet of you, but since I've lived there for thirty-some years now, I'm pretty sure I can find it." She stopped. "Unless you need to talk? The pressures on Charlotte surely spill over on you."

"Me?" Julie nearly squeaked. "Oh, no. No, I'm fine, really. Charlotte handles her job very well."

"As her mother, I appreciate the contributions you make to her welfare. You have a good evening, dear."

"You, too, Mrs. Marchand." But Julie's voice sounded sad enough that as Anne rode up in the elevator, she resolved to check in with the girl tomorrow and make sure she was really all right.

She was still thinking about Julie when she opened her door.

And found all four of her daughters inside.

"Well, now. Have I forgotten an occasion?"

Then their expressions registered. Charlotte's was grim, Melanie's furious, Renee's determined and Sylvie's sad.

"What's wrong? Daisy Rose is okay? *Grand-mère?* Or is it Pete or—"

Sylvie was beside her. "Everyone's fine, Mama." She cast a chastening glance at her sisters. "Great job, girls. Scare her to death." She turned back to Anne. "We just need to talk to you."

"About what?" Whatever it was couldn't be good. "If it's not the family, what's happened with the hotel?"

"Mama, sit down. Please." Charlotte approached her, arms stiff by her side, as if she were facing a firing squad.

Then a bolt of pure fear hit her. "William. He's hurt. He's—" Blindly, she sought the door.

Sylvie gripped her hand. "William is healthy, as far as we know. Please sit, Mama."

Anne tugged her hand away. Rubbed her arms, suddenly cold. Her stomach took a long, greasy roll. Even without hearing more, she felt some part of her already alert for danger. For pain.

"I prefer to stand." She held herself erect, bracing for the blow. "Whatever you have to say, don't string it out."

But Charlotte, her strong, steady Charlotte, had tears in her eyes. "Mama, I'd sell my soul not to have to tell you this. I considered every option because I'm scared to death of hurting you or harming your health. But I knew, in the end, that only the truth would suffice."

"Stop dragging your heels, Charlotte Anne. I'm not going to have another heart attack. Spit it out." She hated to be so brusque with one of her babies, but a deep, nasty ache was settling into her bones.

Charlotte glanced around at her sisters as if for strength, then exhaled in a weary gust. "William is the one who made the second offer on the hotel. I just found out today."

At first, Anne thought she was hearing things. "What? No, he couldn't have— He wouldn't—"

We have another offer for the hotel. From a new party.
His eyes had only been concerned. *Who is it?*
No. Please, no.
Would it be so wrong to accept the offer?

I love you, Anne.

His voice, the thrill she'd felt, mocked her now.

She fought off sick dread.

"No." She clutched her fingers more tightly on her crossed arms. "He…" Loves me. *I love you, Anne.*

Blue eyes gazing into hers as he bent to her. Caressed her. Held her when she faltered.

"You're wrong, Charlotte. However did you make this leap? Did you ask him?"

For a second, her daughter looked uncertain. "I didn't have to. I asked Jud Lawson's assistant."

"The trustee."

Charlotte nodded.

"And the assistant confirmed it?"

"Next thing to it."

"What would make you do such a thing in the first place?" Anne felt rebellious. Images of William's kindness flew at her, shutter-fast.

Holding her.

Listening to her.

Laughing with her.

Making love.

The man who'd done those things couldn't have deceived her this way. Charlotte must be wrong. "You didn't want me seeing William, and I understand the dilemma. You and your father were so close. Of course it's hard to think of me with another man, but you would stoop to spying on William?"

Her daughter reacted as if she'd slapped her. "I didn't spy. Someone left me a note."

"Who?"

"It was anonymous."

"Well, then." Anne felt steadier. "Maybe the Corbins had that sent to you, to rattle you so that we would quit considering the second offer."

"I spoke to Jud Lawson, too, Mama." Charlotte's tone was laced with pity.

"And he admitted it?"

"Not in so many words. Legally, he can't. But I read between the lines. There's no question, Mama."

Anne turned away from her children. Between those lines lay her future. Her heart. "So you can't be certain."

"Judith Armstrong was in my office just a little while ago. Feeling me out about terms."

Anne wondered then exactly how many ways there were for a heart to break. But she persisted. "So maybe Regency Corp. made the offer without William's knowledge."

"Mama, William *is* Regency." But Charlotte's expression betrayed some doubts. "Actually, in this case, I think it's William who's acting without anyone else at Regency knowing. Judith was stunned when I confronted her."

"So she doesn't believe you, either."

"Oh, Mama," Sylvie said. "I understand why you don't want to credit this, but—"

Her daughters were crowding her, each one looking sorrowful.

She held up a hand. "I need you to leave me alone now."

Their shock was as great as her own. She had never in her life rejected the strong ties that bound them.

"Mama, we're only trying to protect you," Renee said. *I want to take care of you.*

She was suffocating in the intentions of others. "I need time." She clutched her middle. "I don't know what to think."

"I'll call him for you, Mama," Melanie offered. "Tell him to back off."

"No." Anne's refusal brooked no interference. She took in a deep breath and prayed for calm in this maelstrom within her. "I know you all love me, and I love you. You only want what's best for me, and I understand that, but—" Her voice broke. When they moved toward her again, she longed for that circle of love as much as she craved space from it. "Please. I just—"

She looked from face to beloved face, settling on Charlotte's last of all. "I'm sorry. I know this was hard for you. I'll be all right, but I have to handle this myself." She pasted on a smile as only a mother can. "Really. Don't worry about me. I promise I will call you when I'm ready to talk." She eyed her bedroom, wanting to escape and shut herself in, but she couldn't bear to be so restricted.

"Go now, *mes anges*. Mama needs some time alone."

Still they hesitated. "I wish Papa were here," Melanie said, seeming her daddy's little girl again.

"Oh, *bébé*—" The thought of Remy nearly broke her then. "So do I." But she straightened her shoulders and put everything she had into convincing her girls that they weren't abandoning her. It was a mother's job to be leaned on, not to lean. "But he isn't, and I'll be fine. We'll be fine. Now, shoo, and perhaps we'll meet for coffee later, *bon?*"

They were clearly not convinced, but at last it was Sylvie, another mother, who broke the standoff. "All right, girls." She began to herd them through the door. "We'll give her a while—" she cast Anne a meaningful glance "—and then we'll hunt her down like a dog."

Anne's smile became a little more real. "I promise, *chère*. Just a little time."

So they left, but Charlotte was the last. She turned at the door. "I don't think I'm mistaken, Mama, but I wish I were." Remorse weighed her down unmercifully.

"It's never wrong to tell the truth to your mother, *doucette*. Now go. I'll call you in a bit." *If I don't get to be alone in one more minute, I'll shriek. Or weep.*

"I love you, Mama."

"And I you, *mon ange.*"

Still, Charlotte hesitated, only slowly closing the door.

Anne's composure held until she turned the lock, crossed the room.

Walked into her bedroom, seeing William everywhere.

Then she sagged to the floor.

And sobbed her heart out.

CHAPTER THIRTEEN

IN HIS HOME OFFICE, William dictated one more memo for his assistant to type up in the morning, forcing himself not to look at his watch again.

He would see Anne in just over an hour. He had left the office early, too impatient to hang around. And he still had plenty of time to shower and pick her up.

I want to see her now.

He was pathetic. He leaned his chair back, propped his feet on his desk—

And grinned at himself. He'd been more patient when he was sixteen and anticipating his first car date.

He hadn't known beans. Hadn't possessed the first clue what it would be like to love a woman, to make love to her and not simply score. To formulate plans that lasted beyond the next four hours, stretching instead over the next, he hoped, many years.

That young man had had youth on his side and stamina out the wazoo—

But surprisingly enough, William wouldn't trade places with him.

Because that young man's future had been to lose— though he'd never had her, not really—the treasure that was Anne Marchand. No, all William wished he could trade was the span of years ahead of him. He'd love nothing more than to spend forty or fifty years with Anne, but their time together would be much less, no matter how fit they kept themselves. The thought made him more than a little sad.

They would make the most of each precious second, he vowed. Live in the moment the way kids never could, too busy grasping for the future.

Now was what counted. Today. He smiled extravagantly. Tonight.

He wasn't without his future plans, of course. Anne had changed them. He was eager now to settle Judith into his chair and turn over the reins. Help Anne and Charlotte steady their hotel's footing.

So that he could spirit Anne away. Travel, anywhere she wanted. Or stay at home, if that's what she preferred. His only firm requirement was…her. Twenty-four seven. Three-sixty-five. Stretching the time they were allotted to encompass every last pleasure he could give her. Each moment of peace and security and comfort he was allowed to provide.

The front door opened. "Daddy, are you here?"

He sat up. Smiled because he'd just been thinking of his daughter.

She charged through his door, hair disheveled, eyes red.

He surged to his feet. "What's wrong? Are you hurt? Come here, let me look at you—"

She recoiled from him as if he'd slapped her. "How could you?"

His head jerked back. "What? I don't understand."

"I'm the one who doesn't get it." Her face was ravaged. "I thought you trusted me, but you don't, do you? Not if you could keep something like this from me."

It didn't take a genius to figure out what she meant. He was only keeping one secret from her—well, two, if you counted that he'd fallen in love with Anne. "How did you find out?"

"You don't even deny it? I couldn't believe it when Charlotte threw it in my face. I told her you would never—but you have, haven't you?"

Dread settled into his gut. "Charlotte…knows?" Oh, dear God. She would tell— "I have to call Anne."

His daughter crumpled before his eyes. "You betray me, and you're only worried about her? What kind of hold does that woman have on you?" She folded in on herself and sank to a chair. "I'm your child, Daddy."

"Oh, sweetheart." He knelt beside her, though he was desperate to get to Anne before her daughter did. "I didn't betray you."

Her head whipped around. "What did you do, take the offer I structured and submit it without me? Put me off by patting me on the head and sending me to Dallas, so I would think you actually had confidence in me?"

"Oh, honey, no. It wasn't that way at all. I do have confidence in you. You're going to take over, and you'll be good at it—"

She shoved to her feet so abruptly that he nearly lost his balance. She stood over him, a virago with eyes shining fury. "You gave me this job because you pitied me. I couldn't even do a good job of being a wife, much less running the company you love more than me. And now you've made a fool of me. Don't appease me. This isn't a scrape you can kiss and make better."

He rose to his full height. Reminded himself that she was still shaky and emotional after the divorce. "You're wrong," he said quietly. "And if you'll quit being hysterical, I'll explain everything to you."

But she was beyond reason. "I wish Mother had lived instead of you. She would never, ever—" Judith nearly spat the words "—have done this to me. She loved me. Was always there for me."

He couldn't deny that Isabel had been the more hands-on parent. But that didn't mean he didn't love Judith. Wouldn't like to cut out his own heart at the moment. "I love you, too, Judith. I never meant to hurt you." He reached out for her.

She pulled away. Her devastated eyes raked scores over his conscience. "But you did."

"Honey, sit down and let's talk."

She wheeled toward the door. "I—I can't talk now. I'm very tired." Her voice was small, like a child's.

"Judith, come back here." He started after her.

She picked up her pace until she was running.

Away from him.

William watched her go and wondered why his best intentions had gone so wrong. In trying to save the woman he loved, had he sacrificed, intentionally or not, the daughter he'd loved far longer?

He stood very still for endless seconds, torn between

racing after the child who wanted nothing to do with him—and going to the woman who might very well come to agree completely with her.

He reminded himself that even as a child, Judith had been more receptive when given time to cool down. Her temper was quick, but she didn't hold grudges.

He swallowed the sorrow that was his worry for his daughter, and sped toward the telephone. He would call Anne and hope to heaven that he caught her before Charlotte did. He would explain everything, and she would see that he'd only wanted to help her.

Or, as he'd feared when he'd taken the gamble, she would not. But he'd stay after her until her temper eased. Until she forgave him.

And the very first second that his daughter indicated a willingness to listen, he would do the same with her.

Somehow he would make all this work out. He had a knack for it.

But as he punched Anne's number into the phone, the thrill he'd always gotten from flying in the face of risk felt a lot more like an endless plunge into a dark, gloomy cavern.

Anne's phone rang and rang until her voice mail picked up. He glanced at his watch. Even a woman who'd proven her speed at dressing would be getting ready by now.

He hung up without leaving a message.

And paced as he wondered where she was.

ANNE HEARD the phone ring, and every peal of it was a stone casting ripples, each one spreading a wider circle edging toward her. Almost, but not quite, touching the stillness she'd willed around herself after she'd cried harder than any time in her life except the moment she'd accepted that Remy was truly gone.

She'd gathered that same silence around her in those awful days, and it had kept her going through the funeral and the first ragged wounds of her children's grief. And when she'd finally cried, she'd done so alone, deep in the night after everyone had finally let her be by herself.

Solitude could be healing. It was a necessary part of life; each person was, in the end, alone.

She'd accepted that. Made her peace with it.

Then had come William. Even now, it was a cruel irony that the person she wanted most to talk to about the pain that lay in wait to tear at her was the man who had caused it.

Had she, just hours before, treasured the luxury of someone in whom to confide?

Her laugh was a raw scrape up her throat. She'd confided, all right. No wonder the new offer had seemed so perfect.

But even now, gratitude wanted to stir. The offer had been generous; both she and Charlotte had acknowledged that. Marveled at their fortune, even as they'd vowed not to accept.

He'd made a fool of her. He hadn't been able to resist the opportunity to own Remy's dream, after all.

But it had been her dream, too. And he'd kissed her, held her...made her feel cherished.

She sat up on the mattress.

For God's sake, at least let me do this.

Was it possible? Could he have—

There weren't enough ways to express how wrong his move had been, but—

The man who'd loved her so tenderly, who'd champed at the bit to take action on her behalf, that man was capable of a gesture he would see as bolstering her position.

Be honest, Anne. That's exactly what it did.

She stood up and wobbled, dizzy from a stuffy nose after all those tears. She had to talk to him. Find out the truth.

Oh, please. Let Charlotte be wrong.

She made for the bathroom to wash her face, restore her makeup. At the sink, however, she faltered. Stared into the mirror.

Was she honestly ready to deal with a man again? Give him entry into her life? She'd adored Remy, but any relationship required work and compromise.

William was a full-grown man with his own habits and preferences and needs. Even if she weren't kidding herself by assuming this offer wasn't about double-dealing to achieve a goal, the truth remained that he'd lied to her. Just how well did she know him, anyway, if he could see her as someone to work around rather than a woman who could stand on her own?

Because she could. Had. If he could pay lip service to her strength but not respect it, then they were in for a rough ride.

And if the truth were worse, and he'd actually deceived her, seduced her as a means to an end—

She shoved away from the counter. He was due here in thirty minutes, and she couldn't wait that long to find out. Too much was at stake.

She crossed into her living room. Stared at the phone. Rejected it.

This was a conversation to be had in person.

Let him look her in the eye and explain himself.

Then they would see if there was anything to be made of this attraction between them. He could not love her and lie to her, not now.

At the door, she paused. Steadied her breath. Searched for the strength that had brought her this far in her life.

She was afraid of what she would hear, yes.

But there would be truth between them.

Or there would be nothing.

BLOUNT'S CELL PHONE RANG, disturbing his poker game. "What?" he barked.

"Something's up at the hotel, boss."

His trusted lieutenant. "Explain."

"Ricky was checking out spots for the fire, just like you asked, while I was keeping tabs on the Marchand woman. She gets around a lot, you know that? Talks to a lot of people."

"Like who?"

"You know. Tourists and stuff. Everybody's crazy about her."

Blount rolled his eyes. "I'm in the middle of something here. Get to the point."

"Oh. Yeah, well, remember you told us to pay attention

to that guy Carter? The one working for Dumb and Dumber?"

Blount's mouth twitched. The Corbins sometimes did resemble the bozos in that movie, but it didn't pay to underestimate them. "So what's he doing?"

"He saw Ricky. Bumped into him. Watched him some." When Blount didn't say anything, he continued. "We're wondering if someone told him about the plans for the fire."

Blount counted to ten. "They'd better not have. I don't trust those two to carry it off. That's why I put Ricky and you in there to make sure the damage is limited."

"Think we should pay him a visit, see what he knows?"

Blount wondered if the Corbins could be so rash as to share the details of their business with someone under them. If so, Carter would have to be taken care of.

But not yet. "Keep an eye on him. See if he does anything funny. I wouldn't put it past those two to try an end run around us. Not that they'd succeed, but we don't need anything screwing up this close to the end. That all?"

"Uh, no. There's more."

"Like what?"

"Something's got the daughters all upset. The whole bunch went to their mother's quarters, and when they left, some of them were crying."

Blount smiled. "Maybe they see the writing on the wall. Know they have to sell."

"Guess so. But then Mrs. Marchand was in there a long time, but now she's leaving in that hot Corvette she drives."

"So?"

"I heard Armstrong say he'd pick her up at seven."

"It's six-thirty."

"Maybe their plans changed, but she didn't look happy. Oh, and the tap you got on that lawyer's phone?"

"Lawson."

"Right. Well, Jackie says Charlotte Marchand knows about Armstrong's offer."

"Hmm."

"Yeah. And Armstrong's daughter paid her a visit this afternoon."

Armstrong's daughter and Marchand's daughter. What were they cooking up? "I don't like it."

"What do you want us to do, boss?"

The Corbins were losing control of the situation, that much was obvious. They needed to be cut out of the pack and isolated before everything went to hell. "Who's on the Corbins?"

"Lou's on Dan, Sally's on Richard."

"Find out what they're doing and bring them in."

"You got it."

"And tell everyone, eyes sharp on the Marchands."

ACROSS TOWN, Dan Corbin listened to a message from his brother. "Charlotte Marchand and Judith Armstrong met this afternoon. They're going to cut us out of this, bro. Or Blount will. I tried it your way, but can't wait any longer. I'm taking action."

"Holy hell, Richard," he murmured. "What have you done?" He punched his brother's cell phone number.

The phone went direct to voice mail.

ANNE WAITED for the valet to retrieve her car for her and stared sightlessly into the distance. She should probably wait for William to arrive and have a calm discussion about Charlotte's news. Give him a chance to explain his thinking.

But she didn't feel the least calm. The more she considered, it didn't matter if he were deceiving her for a beneficent reason or a malevolent one.

Deceit was deceit. He knew—he *knew* how she felt about the topic. Hadn't she poured her heart out about what Remy's dream meant to all of them? How critical it was to her and her girls that they preserve the work of nearly forty years?

Her work, damn it. She'd labored alongside Remy, strained herself nearly to the bone. Juggled family and business, worrying every second that she'd fail both. That she couldn't be enough for everyone she loved.

William was accustomed to getting his own way. To ruling his world. Master of all he surveyed.

And love was something, yes. Something big. But respect was as critical.

By the time she'd reached his house, her anger was a slow, smoldering coal, ready to ignite with only a faint breath.

She parked the Corvette on the street. Strode up the walk. Averted her gaze from the spot on the porch where she'd kissed him.

Giggled with him when they'd been caught.

The door opened before she could knock.

He looked…guilty. Unsettled.

"I tried to call you."

She shrugged. "I'm here. Beat you to the punch."

He went silent while he examined her. Looking, perhaps, to assess her mood.

She couldn't speak herself. The sight of him brought too many memories rushing in. Making her question every last one of them.

The moment was still…but not empty. Pregnant with the sense that everything could change, here and now. That what had been between them could vanish with a word. Her ears wanted to pop with the pressure of it, as on a plane, during ascent, when simple air seems unlikely to bear the weight of all the hopes and plans of the passengers.

"Will you come in?" he said with extreme politeness.

"No. I don't—" Hated moisture hovered there, just behind her eyes. He wasn't rushing to deny any of it. "I can't. Not after what you've done."

Astonishingly, though, his chin jutted. "Why don't you tell me exactly what you think that is."

Unbelievable. Her mouth gaped. "You defend it?"

His arms crossed over his chest. "I do."

She snapped her mouth shut. Shook her head. "Are you sorry?"

"If I hurt you, yes. But it was necessary."

She shook her head to be sure she was hearing right. "You truly don't understand me, do you? You don't have the slightest sense of who I am. What's important to me."

"You're wrong about that," he said softly. But no penitence.

She stared at him. "So you were aware, but you decided you knew better."

"Anne, sometimes—"

"Answer me. You heard me tell you, over and over, that I wanted—no, needed, to handle this myself. But King William, empire builder, decided that the little woman couldn't—or shouldn't, doesn't matter— possibly manage to work her way out of a fix, so he set his own plans into motion."

"You make me sound like a villain. I was only trying to protect you."

She could draw little comfort from knowing that she was right and Charlotte was wrong about his motives. "So you and your daughter weren't playing some game with Charlotte and me?"

He frowned. Looked guilty again. "Judith proposed an idea, but I…" He shook his head. "Never mind. It's not important."

"Not important? Just as what I needed, what I wanted, wasn't? You sat there, you listened to me, you— held me, for God's sake, and dried my tears, all the while hatching your own plot?"

"Anne, that's unfair. I was only—"

"Unfair?" The flames flared in one quick spark. "You lied to me, William. You told me you loved me—"

"I do love you," he interrupted.

"—and deceived me with every breath."

"Deceive is a harsh word, Anne."

She threw up her hands. "I'm leaving before this gets ugly."

"Ugly?" A strained laugh escaped. "This isn't? You throw my love in my face? Discard everything good between us because I tried to help you? You expect me to love you and just stand by with my hands in my pockets? I protect those I love, Anne. It's who I am."

"I can't talk to you now, William." She turned to go, her legs shaky. She had to focus on each step as she struggled to maintain some sense of dignity.

He followed her. Clasped her arm and began to turn her. "Anne, don't do this. Calm down and we can reason this out. I'm sorry that you're hurt—"

She wheeled on him. "But are you sorry you did it?"

His gaze ranged over her features, and she could see the war in him.

Abruptly, she decided she couldn't bear to hear his answer.

So she tore herself away.

And ran.

WILLIAM ITCHED to go after her, but he was honestly unsure if it would help. Maybe he should give her some time instead, no matter how much he yearned to take her in his arms and restore them to the footing they'd had.

But somehow he couldn't stop himself from following her steps. Watching her until she was out of sight.

She got in the car. Lowered her face to her hands. Her shoulders shook.

Screw it. He would go to her, anyway. Do whatever was required to make her see why he'd done it. Hell, he'd apologize. Give her the answer she wanted. Even though he would do the same thing again, in similar circumstances.

She started the car. The best thing that had ever happened to him was driving away from him, and he couldn't bear it. They'd shared laughter and the beginnings of love. Somehow he would make her see. She could yell at him, rain down curses on his head, just—

Forgive me, Anne. Please. It was a calculated risk. And I lost. But I can't lose you.

He took a shortcut through his yard, hidden behind a privet hedge for a few seconds.

He heard a scream. Frowned and sped up. Emerged from a gap in the shrubbery and caught a glimpse that nearly stopped his heart. "Hey!"

The door of her car gaped open.

A man was dragging Anne from it.

She was fighting him, but she was so small.

"Anne," William shouted, and began to run. "Let her go—"

The man whirled and spotted him.

Anne scraped her nails down his face.

He cuffed her on the side of the head. Hard.

She clung to the car. Kicked at him.

"Anne, let go. Let him take it," William shouted. "It's only a damn car."

The man shot a glance at him. Seemed to change his mind and shoved at her.

If he got her inside— *Dear God, help her.*

William had run for exercise for many years, but right now, his legs seemed to be pushing through molasses as he stretched out to close the gap. His lungs burned with the strain, but he couldn't let her be trapped in that vehicle. He'd never be able to catch them.

Just as the man grabbed Anne again, she gouged at his eyes.

He screamed and dropped her.

William poured everything he had into narrowing the distance.

The man rose awkwardly. Aimed a kick into Anne's side where she lay.

A howl like a berserker rose in William's throat.

She was scrambling to rise when the man wheeled in William's direction, something in his hand.

William leaped. Spotted the muzzle flare.

A blow to his chest felt like he'd been rammed by an elephant.

"Anne—" *I love you*, he tried to say.

But everything went black.

CHAPTER FOURTEEN

ANNE CRAWLED toward William, sobbing his name.

"Bitch," her attacker screamed. "Look what you made me do."

She scooted as fast as she could to get between him and William, even though the rage on his face terrified her. "Get away from him." Something resembling a growl emerged from her throat.

He started in her direction. "You will pay for—"

"What's going on here?" A new voice. "I've called the cops. You'd better let her go or—"

She saw the gun rise again, toward the neighbor. Gathered her strength and shoved him.

He grabbed her hair and took her down with him.

Sirens screamed in the distance.

"Goddammit—" The man cast her aside. Leaped to his feet. "This isn't finished, bitch."

He ran to a car parked just down the block and took off.

"Are you all right, lady?"

"Help…get him help," she pleaded as she crawled over to William.

The police arrived. "Back. Everyone back—"

"There's a man who's been shot," her rescuer said.

"Call EMS, Charlie," one cop said, racing to her side. "Ma'am, I need to look at him."

But Anne couldn't leave him. "I can't tell if there's a pulse. He's hurt. He's so hurt." She brought her face to his. "William. Oh, love, please—"

William's lashes stirred.

"Ma'am, please move aside."

She scooted around but couldn't let his hand go. There was blood, so much blood. "William," she whispered. "I'm sorry. I'm so sorry. I love you. Please don't leave me."

For a second, his eyelids parted. The blue was so hazy that she couldn't be sure he saw her.

"You're going to be okay," she said, though she couldn't imagine how he would be. "You hold on. Stay with me, William."

His lips parted, but no sound emerged.

"Don't talk. Oh, don't talk. I'm here. I won't leave you. Please—" she bit back a sob "—stay with me, William. I need you. I'm sorry, so sorry that we—"

His eyes slid shut.

"Ma'am," said a new voice. "I'm a paramedic. I have to ask you to step back. I can't save him if you won't give him to us."

"If I let go, I'll lose him. I lost Remy when I wasn't there. Maybe if I'd—"

A hand to her shoulder. "Move around to his head, then. Talk to him but don't touch, just until I'm done." All the while, competent hands moved over William's body. Incomprehensible terms were tossed about.

Anne knelt behind William's head, restless and

itching to make contact. She gripped her hands tightly to still the trembling and keep from breaking her promise, haunted by the memory of the awful words she'd flung at him only minutes before.

Please, she prayed with everything in her. *Don't let those be the last words we say to each other.*

You make me sound like a villain. I was only trying to protect you.

A sob erupted, acid in her throat.

No, my love, you're a hero. And I'm so scared I'll never get to tell you.

Tell him now, ma belle, said a voice in her head that could have been Remy's. And nearly broke her.

She shivered with fear but kept digging until she found steel. She swallowed hard and squared her shoulders.

Bent to William's ear. "You saved me, William, just as you were trying to protect me before. I'm sorry, so sorry I didn't stay and let you explain." Her voice cracked. She took a second to recover. "But I'll listen to every word, I swear it. Put my pride aside and trust you. Let you have your turn to yell—" Her nostrils flared as she mastered another sob.

"I love you, William Armstrong. Stay with me. Give me the chance to tell you. Please."

"Okay, ready for the gurney. On three—" The paramedics loaded William and turned to race him to the ambulance.

"Where—" She ran to catch them. "Where will you take him?"

One of them glanced back. "You want to go?"

"Yes." She nodded through her tears.

"I need to talk to her," said the cop named Charlie.

She turned anguished eyes on him. "Please. I'll tell you anything, but—"

His eyes were kind as he nodded. "We'll meet you at Mercy. Get yourself looked at, too, ma'am."

"Let's haul," shouted one of the paramedics. "Call it in."

Anne scrambled inside.

The paramedic turned to her. "If you'll stay back about hip-level on him, you can hold his hand."

The tears she'd been fighting spilled over then. She groped through the haze of them, feeling for William's hand.

And held on tight, praying with every cell of her body, as the sirens screamed through the night.

Please. He's a good man. And we've only just found each other.

Don't take him from me.

CHARLOTTE PACED her office.

How long was enough when a heart is broken?

If she lived to be a thousand, she'd never forget the look on her mother's face.

She'd put it there. *I had to tell her, didn't I?*

"Second-guessing?" Sylvie said from the doorway.

Charlotte sought her sister's gaze. "I was wrong, wasn't I?"

"About what? Protecting a woman who's been hurt enough?"

"But I hurt her, maybe the worst."

Sylvie snorted. "You always had delusions of grandeur."

"It's not funny."

Sylvie's eyes were soft. "No. No, it's not." She crossed Charlotte's office. "He's the one who did the damage, sweetie."

Charlotte clenched her fingers. "Maybe I shouldn't have told her. Should have confronted him instead. Told him to stay away."

"So she'd just wonder why he'd dumped her? That's really going to make her feel great."

"I don't know." Charlotte pinched her nose. "I just— I can't stand thinking about her, the expression on her face when I—"

Sylvie glanced at her watch. "I call it time. You're not going to be able to settle down—none of us are—until we check on her."

"You think?"

"Wow, you really are shaken. Big sis, asking my opinion. Be still, my heart." She grinned.

"Smart-ass."

Sylvie smoothed a hand over Charlotte's hair. "Mama's going to be okay. She's incredibly strong."

"Yeah. I hope." Charlotte called out to Julie as they passed. "Tell Renee and Melanie we're headed to Mama's quarters. And you call my cell if something comes up."

"Will do," Julie said. "Hug her for me."

Sylvie made small talk all the way down the hall and up the elevator, but Charlotte barely heard a word. At her mother's door, she sucked in a deep, steadying breath.

And knocked. "Mama?"

No answer.

Knocked again. "It's Sylvie and Charlotte. Please, just tell us you're okay."

They exchanged uneasy glances.

"Do we go in?" Sylvie asked.

"I don't know. What if she's asleep or something?"

At that moment, the elevator dinged, and Melanie and Renee rounded the corner. "She all right?" asked Renee.

"She's not answering."

"Go in," Melanie urged. "We all have the keys she gave us."

Charlotte debated, then pulled out her phone. "I want to respect her privacy." The phone rang until voice mail picked up. "Oh, no." Her fingers suddenly wouldn't work as she fumbled with her key.

"Here, let me." Melanie, ever impatient, pushed past the others and managed the lock.

When the door swung open, for an instant, all four of them hesitated, as if bad news lay inside.

Then Charlotte shook herself and stepped over the threshold. "Mama?" When no answer came, she moved ahead, terrified of what they might find.

No one in the bedroom, only the imprint, in the delicate curve of a sea creature, of their mother's body on the spread.

"She's not in the bathroom," Renee announced. "So where is she?"

"She's gone to him," Sylvie said. "She never takes the easy path. She'd want to confront him herself."

"So do we follow?" Melanie asked. "I can't stand waiting."

Everyone looked to Charlotte.

At that moment, her cell chirped. Every one of them jumped.

"Charlotte Marchand," she answered.

"I don't know how to tell you this," Julie said. "Mercy Hospital just called. It's your mother."

Charlotte's knees gave way. "Oh, dear God. Is she—"

"They won't give me the information. They want to talk to you."

"Give me the number." With shaking fingers, she punched in the digits while her sisters crowded round, asking questions she couldn't answer.

Oh, Mama. Oh, Mama, what have I done to you?

After what felt like years, she was transferred to the nursing station. She listened carefully, all the while staring into her sisters' frightened eyes.

Then she disconnected.

"Mama's been hurt. An attempted carjacking, they think."

Melanie made a sound of distress. She was the one who'd insisted their mother not sell the Corvette.

Sylvie began to cry, and Charlotte wanted to join her.

"She's going to be okay," she managed. "She was beaten up pretty badly, but apparently, she put up quite a fight. But—"

"What?" Renee demanded.

"It's William. He was shot, defending her. And he may not make it."

A stunned silence strung out.

Then Melanie spoke, though her voice was shaky. "I'll get my car. Meet you downstairs."

JUDITH WAS PACKING up her office and weeping at the same time. How could he? Tears raged through her at intervals, and she knew her father would counsel her to wait before making such a sweeping decision.

But her father's advice meant nothing to her now. Had he ever really loved her or only considered her a burden? Pitied her or honestly cared?

Of course, he said he loved her, but how could he, if he'd pull something like this? She paused to blow her nose, then started through the next drawer of her desk.

"Judith."

She glanced up. "Glen?" Oh, great. Her humiliation was complete. "You probably wonder why—" She indicated the boxes.

He crossed to her. "Judith," he said again, and his tone sank in on her with a shiver.

"What is it?"

He gripped her upper arms. "It's your father. He's been shot."

Her eyes flew wide open. "Shot? But what— Who would— Is he—how badly is he hurt?"

"Come on. I'll drive you to Mercy." With an arm around her shoulders, he started to walk.

"No. Tell me. It's bad, isn't it?" She covered her mouth. "Is he—" She couldn't say it.

"He's alive, but his condition is critical. They're taking him into surgery."

"Oh, Glen. I just—" She started shaking. "He—we—we had a terrible fight. Oh, God, if he dies—"

"Your father is tough. If anyone can pull through, he will."

"Oh, God, oh, God—" She started searching for her car keys. "I have to get to him."

"I'm having a car brought around front." Glen took her arm and steadied her as she broke into sobs. "Hold on, Judith. He's going to be okay. We have to believe it."

If I lose him, I will never forgive myself.

Terrified and shaking, Judith let Glen lead her out.

CHAPTER FIFTEEN

ANNE PUSHED BACK the blanket the nurse had placed on her when she couldn't stop shivering and slipped down from the gurney she'd been left on while waiting for her X-rays to come back.

She was halfway across the floor of the cubicle on her way to ask again about William when the drapes flew back—

And her girls rushed to surround her.

"Mama—oh, Mama, where are you hurt—"

"What are you doing out of the bed?"

They surrounded her, all talking at once, her girls, and she clutched at them for strength. "I'm all right," she soothed.

"You're not. Look at you. You're all bruised, and—"

All of them were worried, but Charlotte was a wraith. "Mama, I'll never forgive myself. What have I done?"

Anne reached for her and stifled a gasp when Charlotte hugged her tight.

"Oh. Oh, I'm so sorry. Where are you hurt?"

"I'm fine. Just sore. Come here."

Gingerly, Charlotte complied. She held her mother carefully and pressed their heads together. "Mama, I—"

"Hush," she said. "Not a word of that. I can't think about any of it now. I have to find someone to tell me what's going on with William." Realizing Charlotte would do better with a mission, she gave her one. "Get me out of here, Charlotte."

"We'll take you home, Mama," Sylvie said.

"No. I'm not leaving until I know if William—" She swallowed a lump the size of North America. "He has to make it. I only want out of this—gown. I want my clothes. I need—" Her voice cracked. "I need to be with him."

"But he's in surgery," Melanie pointed out.

"I know. But I have to be as close as I can get." She pinned her eldest. "Talk to them, Charlotte Anne."

Charlotte nodded. "As good as done." She left, and Anne knew that nothing short of God himself would stop her.

Relief made her head light. She swayed.

"Mama!" Renée steadied her. "Get back in bed."

"No. I—"

"Please," said Sylvie. "Just until Charlotte springs you." With a move as smooth as any she'd ever managed herself, Sylvie had her back in the bed before she realized what had happened. "Have they run tests?"

"That's what they're waiting on, X-rays and blood work. But it's been forever."

"I'll go see what I can find out about William," Renee offered.

"Oh, *chère,* thank you. And hurry back, please. He— he was shot, saving me."

"Can you tell us what happened?" Melanie asked.

Renee's steps slowed.

"Please, *chère,* go on. I'll tell it all again, but I have to—" Tears filled her eyes. "He has to make it. I love him."

Renee nodded and left.

Sylvie's own eyes were bright. "Oh, Mama…"

"He's a good man. He wasn't doing anything underhanded. I'm certain of that now." She blinked to clear her vision. "I should have been all along. He was only protecting me. He's very strong-willed and accustomed to taking charge. I don't say I wasn't angry, because I was, but—" She covered her lips. Bit them. "Oh, please," she whispered. "Please give me a chance to take it back."

Sylvie and Melanie flanked her, squeezing her hands. Stroking her hair. "Shh, Mama," Sylvie said. "Let's pray for him, shall we? We can hear the story later."

Anne gripped their hands tightly and took comfort in the sound of Sylvie's voice. The three of them huddled in silence, then, and slowly, Anne's terror receded. She was borne up by her daughters' love and felt faint stirrings of hope.

The girls settled, each on one side of her, the warmth of their bodies seeping into the chill of her own.

And Anne offered up silent pleas for the return of the man she wanted more time to love.

IT FELT LIKE DAYS but was less than an hour before Charlotte worked her magic.

An odd sensation, for a mother, to be dressed by the children for whom she'd once performed the service, but Anne was too sore to manage by herself.

And there was a soothing that came from simple human touch. It could sweep right past words to the heart of things.

Renee popped in again, this time with a fragment of news. "He's still alive, Mama. They hope it won't be much longer before the surgeon comes out."

"Thank you," Anne murmured. "Oh, thank you." She held out a hand to Renee. "I can't tell you how much it helped to have you up there." She looked around. "I'm going upstairs." She waited for objections.

Their faces were grim, but, as so often before, her daughters ranged themselves around her.

And, whatever they believed of William, offered her their full support.

JUDITH WAS PACING the surgical waiting room. Glen had left to make some phone calls, as cell phones weren't allowed in this part of the hospital.

It was just as well. She was useless for small talk, and no one would tell her anything.

Except that her father was still alive.

When the door opened, she whirled, hoping for news—

But stopped in shock. She had never met Anne Marchand, but she'd seen her pictures.

The woman in the doorway was battered and hardly the elegant creature one would expect, but there was a dignity about her still.

And if Judith had had any doubts about her identity, the blazing eyes of Charlotte Marchand and her sisters would have cleared them. Judith didn't move, uncertain how to feel. From what the police had told her, her father had been shot trying to rescue this woman from an attempted carjacking, yet he'd inexplicably tried to buy her hotel from under her. To make matters more confusing, when Judith had confronted him, he'd seemed more concerned about Anne's reaction than her own.

The awkward silence stretched out.

Then Anne Marchand came toward her.

"Mama—" Charlotte reached out as though to stop her.

"I'll be fine," Anne murmured. She made her way with slow steps, obviously in physical pain.

But her eyes revealed pain of another sort. Judith had no idea what to say to her.

Anne took her hand. "You're Judith. William has told me how proud he is of you."

Judith's eyes swam with tears.

"He saved my life. I was—" Anne's own eyes were wet. "I was awful to him, and he still—" Her hand squeezed Judith's.

Judith squeezed back. "So was I."

Anne looked startled for a second, then spoke again. "Whatever is tangled between our families, right now we have something very important in common, and it overshadows all else. You must be frightened, and so am I. Will you sit with me, Judith, and we'll keep vigil together for a man we both love?"

Her words were said with such emotion, such reverence, that Judith found herself leaning into Anne's quiet strength. "I can't think," she admitted. "If he dies—"

"He won't," Anne said firmly. "We have to believe that. I won't lose him."

Judith was reminded that this woman had lost a man she loved once before. This must be incredibly painful for her, waiting and not knowing—

"Please." She gestured to the chair beside her. "Won't you sit down? I'd—I'd like very much to wait with you. If—" She cast a glance at a frowning Charlotte. "If you think your daughters won't mind. I don't really understand all that's going on with your hotel and The Regency, but—"

"Shh, dear." Anne, though several inches shorter than her, patted Judith's shoulder and made her feel cherished. "None of that matters in the face of William's struggle." Her voice wobbled, but her shoulders were straight, her eyes kind and comforting. "Everything else can be worked out later." Gently, Anne sat and drew Judith with her.

Then she looked at her daughters. "Renee, please see if you can find us tea, would you? Sylvie, who is with Daisy Rose?"

"Jefferson has her."

"Good for him. Melanie, does Robert know where you are?"

Melanie smiled. "I'll call him, now that you're okay."

"She's not okay," Charlotte challenged. "She should be home in bed."

Anne arched one eyebrow. "But I'm not. Should you be back at the hotel?"

"They know how to reach me. Julie and Luc are

staying late and dissuading the entire hotel staff from charging over here to check on you."

"I'll bet none of you have had dinner." She turned to Judith. "Are you hungry, dear?"

Judith shook her head. "I couldn't."

Anne smiled sadly. "Nor I." She glanced over at her daughters. "Why don't you go see what there is for you and your sisters after you call Robert, Melanie."

"You need to eat, too, Mama," Charlotte argued. "You're injured."

"Then you go find something small for me, Charlotte. And Sylvie, you help Melanie carry." With the efficiency of a small general, she dispatched her daughters, however unwilling they were to leave her.

Judith began to see why this woman fascinated her father.

Anne settled into her chair and patted Judith's hand, which she hadn't let go. "Now, there. My girls will come around, *chère,* but for now, we'll just wait by ourselves. Do you want to talk?"

Judith had endured all the strained conversation she could bear, with her nerves screaming. "I don't know what to say, Mrs. Marchand."

Another pat. "Then we won't talk. But I'm here if you change your mind, and please call me Anne. You're not alone, dear. And William will be all right. He's a very stubborn man." Judith could feel her fingers trembling, but Anne's voice was steady and calm.

A little of Judith's panic eased, with this formidable woman at her side. She put some effort into aiding

Anne's attempt to put the best face on things. "He's the strongest person I know."

Anne nodded her approval. "And we're strong women." As if that insured his recovery.

Judith's heart lightened a little. Anne's presence fortified her.

And if anyone up there were listening, she could not imagine that Anne Marchand's will would not make an impression.

Judith drew her first deep breath of the evening.

And squeezed the hand of the woman who obviously loved her father.

Oh, Daddy, come back to me.

She cast a glance at the woman beside her, bruised and battered but resolute. Eyes closed, her lips moving slightly as if in prayer.

Come back to both of us, she amended.

THE NIGHT DRAGGED ON. Anne's food was untouched, her tea barely tasted. Weariness sank deep into her bones, and she was getting stiff from sitting so long.

But she betrayed none of that to the young woman beside her, so frightened for her father, or to her girls, who would surely push for her to go somewhere and lie down.

All Anne could think was that she had been thousands of miles away when Remy was dying, and she couldn't leave William, no matter how long this took. With effort, she tamped down, once again, the panic that wanted to rise into her throat. A thousand times in her memory, she'd heard the shot. Had seen William fall.

Watched his blood soak his clothing. Pool on the ground.

She'd longed to touch him, that thick silver hair only microns away from fingers forbidden to make contact, to stroke him, reassure him. Only her voice was allowed to seek him out, and she'd put all her will into urging him to stay, not to leave her, not to die, though the blood had been everywhere—

Stop it, Anne. She realized she was squeezing Judith's hand nearly as hard as she'd gripped William's in the ambulance. Begging him, cajoling—demanding him to live.

She'd only had that one instant when his eyes had half opened to hope that he heard her. That somehow he knew that she was sorry to her depths, that she would regret forever if their last words had been—

"Ms. Armstrong?" A voice from the doorway.

Judith made a small, frightened sound.

Anne's head snapped up. She rose, along with Judith. Kept pace with her, though her legs would barely move.

Her daughters crowded around her.

She couldn't read the doctor's expression, and her heart stuttered. She found Judith's hand, already grasping for her own.

"Yes?" Judith said, her voice trembling.

"Your father made it through the surgery."

Anne breathed for the first time. "His condition?"

An expression of rue. "The bullet did more damage than it should have, perhaps a combination of the shooter's position and the fact that Mr. Armstrong was apparently leaping at him when the gun went off."

Anne's mind went back to that moment, to William's roar of outrage, the look of determination and fury on his face.

"He was," she confirmed.

"So, it came in at an angle, caught the spleen, pierced the liver and nicked a lung. A lot of bleeding, and a great deal of damage to repair. His condition is very serious. His age is a factor, though the fact that he's kept himself in shape is very much to his advantage."

"But he will live, yes?" She forced herself to ask the question Judith seemed afraid to.

"We're very optimistic. He's survived the worst of it. We'll keep him in ICU at least overnight, then we hope to release him to the surgical floor tomorrow. He'll need to be patient—"

Anne couldn't hear the rest in the clamoring of joy inside her and around her. Judith flung herself into Anne's arms, and Anne held on tight, with her girls surrounding them both.

Charlotte would get her the details later, for no matter how Charlotte felt about William, she would always be there for her mother. Anne hoped for a time when there would be less need for the support, but right now, she was profoundly grateful for every one of her daughters and the love they showered on her.

Unexpectedly, her knees gave way; there was a rush to get her seated.

"Mama—"

"Oh, Mama, are you all right?"

"Get the doctor back, Mel—"

"Mrs. Marchand. Anne—"

Anne heard them all, these daughters she loved, and the young woman who might become another one. But she was too busy to respond in the first instant.

Thank you. Oh, thank you for saving him. Thank you for letting me have him back.

A voice rose inside her head. *Le bon Dieu shines on you, ma belle. He knows a good woman when he sees one.*

Oh, Remy...I don't love you less, she thought.

Mais yeah, my Annie. Of course not. How could you? I am one fine specimen, am I not?

She could see his smile, so wide and beloved.

It's okay, isn't it, Remy?

A warmth spread within her. *It's okay, ma belle. You're a woman meant to be loved.*

"Mama? Are you all right?"

Anne snapped back to the circle of young women huddled around her.

"Yes." She smiled. "Absolutely fine."

"They'll let us in to see him once he's settled in ICU," Judith said. "The two of us, if you'd like to go."

"Oh, indeed I would." She passed a hand over Judith's hair. "Thank you, *chère.*"

Anne's gaze ranged over her daughters. "And after Judith and I see William, perhaps you would take me home."

"About time," Charlotte muttered.

Anne smiled. Turned to Judith. "Would you like to

come with us, *chère?* It's not a night to spend alone. I have no extra bedrooms in my quarters, but we could try to find you a room at the hotel."

Judith glanced around at the others. "You're very kind, but I can't imagine that you have a single room empty, this close to Mardi Gras."

Anne looked to Charlotte.

"Not a one." She hesitated, clearly reluctant. Then she squared her shoulders. "I have an extra bedroom in my house. We have some things to discuss."

Judith met her gesture. "We do, but I don't have all the answers. Only my father can explain everything."

"But we can start."

Judith nodded. "We can. But I think maybe I'll go back…home. To his house."

"Will you be okay there, *chère?*" Anne asked. "It's a very big place."

Judith smiled. "But it's where I grew up. Where I feel closest to him."

"Fine." Charlotte rose. "I'm going to check on the hotel." She crossed to the door, and Anne was tempted to call her back and make her play nice.

But at the door, Charlotte turned. Met her mother's eyes first, then Judith's. "I'm glad he's going to make it," she said.

Anne sniffed back tears of pride. "Thank you, *bébé.*"

"Yes, thank you," Judith chimed in.

ANNE HELD HERSELF upright through sheer force of will as they gained entry to the ICU hall. The corridors were wide and white and the stuff of science fiction.

And cold. She shivered. Judith, beside her, walked like an automaton, staring straight ahead.

Poor girl, all alone. William's parents were dead, and his half sister Lily, a jazz pianist on tour, was stranded in Quebec City by a blizzard. There was a cousin, Jackson, who'd been Charlotte's beau in high school, but he traveled the globe for an aid agency.

Anne slipped her arm through Judith's and received a frightened smile in exchange. "You've never been in here?" she asked.

Judith shook her head.

"Neither have I, but we'll manage."

Judith nodded bravely. "We will."

Anne pressed her palm to the huge metal disc that would open the door and thought how proud William would be of his girl.

The doors swung wide, and sterile white changed to an explosion of hums and dials and murmured voices. Anne sought out the first medical person they encountered. "William Armstrong?"

The nurse glanced at a monitor. "He's in seven—that way," she pointed. "Kevin is his nurse."

They passed three cubicles, each with a forest of equipment so dense that it was hard to make out the body lying so still at the center. *Just keep walking*, Anne reminded herself. *William is at the end of the journey*.

"They don't move," Judith murmured. "They could be dead."

Anne squeezed her arm. "But they aren't. And he won't be, either." She couldn't see a number anywhere. *William, where are you?* She felt dwarfed and weak from the night's events. To think that hours before, she'd been primping for a date—

Her eyes filled, and she blinked madly to clear them. They would have other dates. He would be whole again.

He would, she insisted furiously.

"Ms. Armstrong?" a kind male voice inquired. "I'm Kevin, your father's nurse. And this is—?"

Anne looked up. He was young, so young. "I'm Anne Marchand. William is my—" But what were they? What would they be?

"Mrs. Marchand is my father's companion," Judith said. "My mother is dead, and he would want her here. She's the person he was trying to rescue when—"

Kevin's eyes shifted to Anne. "And you've been injured yourself, am I right?"

"Nothing—" Anne had to clear her throat of the roughness "—nothing at all compared to what—" She blinked again, rapidly.

"I suspect you should be in a bed yourself, but I understand. At any rate, the visit must be limited. Five minutes per hour in ICU, though this late at night, it would be a kindness both to him and yourself to wait again until morning to visit. But that's entirely your call."

He gestured behind him. "Before I take you in, let me familiarize you with the situation. I'm sure all these machines look frightening, but I'll explain what each is

for when we get inside. For now, I need you to understand that Mr. Armstrong is unconscious and won't
likely awaken fully for several hours, due to the effects
of the anesthesia required for surgery. He also has a
breathing tube, so he wouldn't be able to speak to you
anyway, but as with much of what's in there, it's merely
a precaution, allowing his body time to resume normal
functions. All his strength should be directed toward the
job of healing, and what we're doing is merely assuming
some of the duties to allow him to adjust to the impact
of both the gunshot and the surgery to repair the
damage."

He paused. "But it's entirely possible that he can
hear you, whether or not he can respond. And touch is
always helpful to patients. Unfortunately, I'll have to ask
you to glove and gown as a precaution against infection,
but he'll still feel the pressure and warmth of the contact." He smiled. "So—are you ready to see him?"

They both nodded. He gave them disposable gowns
and gloves, and Judith helped Anne out when she found
herself too sore to reach up to tie her gown at the back
of her neck.

Then they were at the door of his cubicle, but Kevin
still blocked their view. "I'll be right outside." He
pointed to a computer on the other side of the glass
wall. "We never leave them unmonitored, and each
patient has his own nurse." He stepped aside.

Anne could see the shape beneath the blankets, so
still. Her gaze traveled up the bed, and she barely
stifled a gasp.

Judith didn't manage. "Oh, Daddy…"

Anne grasped her arm and led her to the bed. Tubes and wires were everywhere, it seemed, and his face—

She'd never seen William so immobile. The dynamic man, so powerful and energetic, was nowhere in sight. A breathing tube was taped to the corner of his mouth, and she could barely connect that mouth to the one that had made her tremble with pleasure.

And his eyes, the beautiful blue of them, were shuttered. The only thing that looked like William was his hair, the mane she'd stared down at from behind his head as he bled his life away in the street.

Oh, beloved. Please return to me.

A sob crowded her throat, but Judith's small moan snapped her back.

"If he can hear us, *chère,* he needs only the positive."

Judith's swimming eyes met hers. She bit her lip and nodded. Turned back to him. "I love you, Daddy. I'm so sorry—" She shook her head abruptly. Drew in a deep breath. "Anne is here with me, and you're going to be fine. You made it through the surgery, and they're taking good care of you."

She glanced at Anne, and Anne nodded her praise.

Judith's hand stole toward his, then gripped. "I'm here, Daddy. I love you so much." Then her head rose. "Here's Anne now." And she backed away.

Gratitude blurred Anne's vision. This magnificent man had raised himself quite a girl. She patted Judith's arm. "Thank you." And moved to take her place.

"William," she began, bending near, sliding her

fingers into his slack hand. So much she wanted to say. Apologies, promises, pleas.

But those would come later. They were her needs, not his.

His daughter might not welcome hearing this, but he had to hear what she'd been so hesitant to say before, until he lay bleeding at her feet.

"I love you, William Armstrong. You say I'm a challenge, but you've—" Her voice cracked. She started again. "You've won, William. I've been afraid to love you, afraid to care that much again, but you—" And here she couldn't help smiling. "You've had your way, as you always seem to do."

She stroked his forehead. Let her touch linger there while her other hand gripped his. "So come on, you empire builder, master this obstacle, too. You conquered me, after all."

She bent and barely stopped herself from kissing his brow in time. She wanted to climb in that bed with him and protect him from everything, shield him and comfort him—

And later, by God, she would.

One more stroke, one more squeeze. "I want more adventures, my love. Come back to your beautiful, brave daughter, William, and please—" she swallowed hard "—come back to me."

"Ladies, I'm sorry, but it's time," Kevin said.

Anne moved aside and let Judith have the last chance.

"I'll be back, Daddy." Then she looked at Anne. "We both will."

Anne smiled through her tears.

CHAPTER SIXTEEN

ANNE COULDN'T SLEEP.

She should be tired enough, certainly—and was. But as the hours passed, her aching body settled into a low scream. She had pain pills, of course, prescribed at the hospital.

But she would not take them. Somehow, she had a sense that she was holding vigil. That she could help tie William to earth, keep him from passing, as Remy had, into another plane of existence, where she could not follow.

But I'm still here, ma belle. Still with you.

Anne shook her head at her foolishness in persisting to hear Remy's voice. *So you've become my guardian angel, have you?* A smile twitched her lips.

Who better? She could swear she heard him say.

She laughed, but it was strained. She'd lost her mind, quite obviously. The stress of everything had accumulated until she'd clearly gone batty.

Well, nothing for it but to get out of bed. She'd always been a big believer in the power of motion to overcome doubt. Sometimes you just had to take a step, even if you weren't sure of your destination, and matters would become clearer.

Her rising wasn't pretty; thank goodness no one was here to see it. She would swear every muscle she possessed, and some she hadn't known existed, was sore and bruised. She shuffled her way to the bathroom and started a shower, hot as she could stand it.

A bath was tempting, but she'd better remain standing. Having to call the desk for help in getting out of the tub would bring her overprotective daughters running.

She remained there for a long time, blessing the huge capacity of their boilers that she had plenty of hot water to restore her muscles to some semblance of flexibility.

As she dressed, she recognized who—and what—she was dressing for.

She was going to see William. Didn't matter if she had to wait fifty-five minutes of each hour to be with him, or if he had awakened. If it was not yet dawn or if her daughters would disapprove or she'd have to negotiate with her staff not to forestall her—

By his side was the only place she wanted to be.

And so she would.

Forty-five minutes later, with reassurances to her staff and messages left for her daughters and Judith, Anne was at the hospital where Kevin, bless him, had not yet gone off duty and had agreed to let her inside.

"Mrs. Marchand, I'm a little surprised to see you back so soon."

"How is he?"

Kevin smiled. "He's been awake twice. Still groggy but coming out of it more each time he wakens."

She gripped his forearm. "That's wonderful. Oh, that's—" She had to duck her head for a minute to gather herself.

"He's doing well enough that I'll talk to the doctor on duty and see if I can clear you to remain in the room as long as you wish."

"Would you?" That's what she wanted, she realized. To be with him from now on. To grab every second.

"There may be times when we'll need to ask you to step out while we tend to him, but, sure—" He winked at her. "There's nothing that helps a patient heal faster than loved ones."

Anne grasped for a tissue from her purse. Blew her nose and dabbed at her eyes as some of the ice inside her melted. "I do love him," she said, looking into the young man's gentle eyes. "He—he's said he wants to marry me, but I—" She stopped. "Well, I don't know why I'm telling you this." She snapped herself into some semblance of her usual composure. "Glove and gown again?"

His expression was kind as he nodded. "For now. Until he's moved upstairs."

"When will that be?"

"I'm sure he won't be here for my next shift. By this afternoon, I'd guess, if he continues to improve." He gestured toward the metal chest containing sterile gowns and boxes of gloves. "Let me just make one check, then he's all yours." He headed off, then turned back. "Oh, and Mrs. Marchand?"

"Yes?"

"I don't get to be with my patients for long, usually, but I do care about them, and I see the effects of this place on their families. Don't be embarrassed that you confided in me. ICU sort of strips everything down to the basics." He smiled. "He's a lucky man to be so well-loved. Not all my patients have that."

"You have a gift, Kevin," she said. "Your patients are fortunate."

"Not all of them make it, Mrs. Marchand. But this one will, I promise." He left her then.

Moments later, she was standing on William's far side, out of the main activity area in his cubicle. Kevin had brought her a chair, but it was too low for William's bed, which was set at a height to allow the staff to tend to him without a lot of bending, Anne guessed. Maybe she would sit in a bit, but for now, she wanted to be as close to William as she could manage.

"William," she said, gripping his right hand. "It's Anne. I'm here. I love you."

The breathing tube had been removed, thank goodness, replaced with a small tube feeding oxygen into his nostrils. She studied the planes and angles of his face. The lines that fanned from his eyes, carved his forehead.

They were not young, either of them. They would not have unlimited years together.

Why on earth had she been willing to waste a second of them?

She smoothed his hair. "I don't know if you can hear me, but they say you might. I am so very sorry, William, for all the terrible things I said to you." She inhaled sharply. "I'm a proud woman, perhaps too proud, and it was never about you, but my need to remain independent. To take care of myself. Too late, I realize that it had everything to do with losing Remy and being afraid to go through that again. It took the heart from me, William. I hurt so badly I thought I would die. I would have, sometimes, gladly, if not for my girls."

She stroked his brow. "I won't try to tell you that I'm not still scared. Nearly losing you—" She had to pause. "It's been as bad as I feared. Losing you would be every bit as devastating as Remy's death. If I had a brain in my skull, I'd run away, far and fast."

She exhaled softly with a sound of rue. "But it appears that whatever brains I had vanished completely when you moved in on me. You did that, William, don't try to deny it. I was another mountain to climb, another battle to win in your quest to dominate the world around you."

She smiled then. "But I'd bet that if you were awake, you'd just give me that shrug of yours, cocky and completely without remorse, wouldn't you? I despair of you, William Armstrong, but—" She gave a small laugh. "I find myself utterly charmed by you. You charged into my life, bent on your goals, and you swept me right off my feet. You made me laugh again, blast you, and you turned my world upside down. I was resigned to being an old lady and only hoping to be graceful in my decline—"

She shook her head. "And what did you do but make me remember what it was to be a woman again, one who was desired? And…loved."

Tears pricked at her eyes again. "I thought I was done with romance, but you saw to that, didn't you?" She bent over. Squeezed his hand and cupped his cheek. "Well, you've done it now. You're all I can think of, all I can see. So you wake up, you big pirate, you. Wake up and let me tell you how much I love you. Give me just one of those too-charming smiles I can't seem to resist."

At that moment, his lids fluttered once.

"Yes," she whispered fiercely. "That's it. Come back. Let me see those devil's blue eyes. You don't even have to talk, not yet. Just…oh, William…" The tears rolled down her cheeks unchecked. "I need you so. Love you so."

Through the blur of her weeping, she saw it then, the flash of blue. She bit her lip. "Yes, my love. I'm here. Please, please, come back."

Then they were there, open but hazy. Scanning her as if trying to place her.

His mouth opened. His voice was a croak. "Anne?"

She covered her gasp. Laughed out her gratitude. "Yes, it's me. Oh, William, I love you so much. You're going to be fine, just fine."

He tried to lick his lips, and suddenly Kevin was there, dipping a sponge on a stick into water and moistening his mouth. William's eyes darted to him.

"I'm Kevin, remember? You're doing fine, Mr. Armstrong. I can't give you water yet, but this will help."

Then he handed the glass and sponge to Anne. "Here. Would you like to do this while I take some readings?"

She nodded, took them gratefully, though she was reluctant to let go of William's hand.

"Anne." His voice was barely a whisper.

"Shh," she said. "You don't have to talk now."

He shook his head impatiently. Winced. "You...okay?"

She dipped her head. Blinked back tears at the joy of hearing him. Of knowing that her welfare was his first thought. "I'm fine, just fine. Now that you're awake, I'm absolutely marvelous."

His eyelids drifted shut. "Tired."

"I know, my love. Sleep now."

"Don't...leave," he murmured.

"Oh, I won't. I promise I won't. And Judith will be back later. She'll be so happy." She placed the glass and its sponge on the bedside table and gripped his hand again. Cupped his cheek. "I'm so very happy to see you."

"Sorry." His gaze sharpened, just for an instant. "Not...want...hurt."

"I'm sorry, too. Please don't worry. Just rest now."

"Love you," he murmured sleepily. "So...much."

"I love you, too, William. Oh, how I love you."

He drifted off with a smile on his face.

Anne sank into the chair.

And wept her profound relief and gratitude.

They would have their chance, after all. She would make the most of every second granted to them.

Kevin caught her gaze and smiled.

Anne smiled back and settled in to wait.

For her future. For the man who was her heart.

ACROSS TOWN, a telephone rang. A sleepy man answered.

"Bring in the Corbins—now," Mike Blount's curt

voice snapped. "And get hold of Ricky and Lou. As of tonight, I'm taking over."

"Yes, sir."

"The Marchand women need a lesson. They'll sign…or else."

* * * * *

HOTEL MARCHAND
Four sisters. A family legacy. And someone is out to destroy it.
Danger makes truth crystal clear

It's the craziest time of year in New Orleans, but Charlotte Marchand has never experienced a Mardi Gras quite like this. Someone on her staff is out to destroy her family's hotel, and as general manager, she can't let that happen. Even the unexpected return of her high school sweetheart, Jackson Bailey, can't completely distract her....

Here's a preview!

THE MARDI GRAS mask was a whimsical concoction of white feathers and sequins. Scarcely longer than Charlotte's hand, it shimmered as it rested on her palm, as weightless—and as fragile—as the trace of a kiss. It was meant to be an adornment, not a disguise, designed to evoke a fairy-tale princess.

Of course, fairy tales were for children, as impractical as make-believe and as implausible as happy endings. A person had to find their own luck, just as they had to guide their own fate. Charlotte Marchand had learned long ago that the real world made no allowance for weaknesses, and she couldn't permit herself any now.

Charlotte blinked, surprised to feel the sting of tears. She pressed her lips together and breathed deeply through her nose until the urge to weep passed. She wouldn't permit herself to fall apart, even here in the privacy of her office. That was a luxury she couldn't afford.

Resolutely she placed the mask on the corner of her desk and focused on the stack of printouts in front of her. It was late, and she'd been at the hotel since daybreak, but she still had work to do before she could go home. Somewhere in that pile of numbers there had to be a solution, and it was up to her to find it.

The week before Mardi Gras was traditionally the busiest tourist season of the year, the make-or-break time for the New Orleans hospitality business. This year more than ever, countless jobs depended on making it a success. But at the Hotel Marchand, bookings were on a downward spiral. The string of problems that had plagued them over the past several weeks had driven away customers and wiped out their profits. The Marchand family finances had been stretched to the breaking point and couldn't prop up the business indefinitely. Charlotte needed to turn things around within the next seven days or the hotel likely wouldn't see another Mardi Gras.

Then again, people flocked to Mardi Gras in order to forget their troubles and cut loose. It was a celebration of possibilities, when anything could happen.

Just this once, why shouldn't it happen for her?

The mask caught the glow of the desk lamp, setting off a flash of sequins. The feathers shifted on some current of air that Charlotte couldn't feel, making it look as if they stirred on their own, as if by magic....

Pressure built in her throat, but she wasn't sure whether it was from more tears or from an irrational urge to laugh.

Magic? Fairy tales? What was wrong with her tonight? Maybe the strain of trying to keep the hotel afloat was finally catching up to her. She never indulged in whimsy. She was sensible, responsible Charlotte, always doing the right thing and obeying every rule. She strove to be a good daughter and granddaughter, sister and aunt, putting others first, whatever the cost.

Fine, that was all well and good, but when was it going to be *her* turn?

The hush of her office was shattered by the shriek of the fire alarm.

Charlotte's hand jerked, knocking the mask to the floor. She grabbed her cell phone and dialed the number for security. "Mac!" She jammed the phone to her ear, trying to hear over the noise of the alarm. "What's going on?"

Mac Jensen was in his last week as head of the hotel's security. "A smoke detector in maintenance was triggered," he replied. His voice was uneven—he sounded as if he were running. "I'm heading there now."

Black smoke puffed through the open bar doors. That explained the mass scramble to evacuate. This was no false alarm.

Charlotte spun from the window and headed for the corridor. At least her family was safe. Her sisters weren't working tonight; lately they had been spending every spare minute with their new fiancés. They were all trusting Charlotte to take care of the hotel....

Between the continuing alarm bleats, she was sure she heard distant sirens. Several of the hotel's uniformed security staff were at the front entrance to keep order outside and to direct the firemen when they arrived. Everything was going according to the emergency plan.

Yet the panic was there, just beneath the surface, and no amount of logic could combat it.

The hotel was more than bricks and mortar to Charlotte, far more than just a means to make a living. It was the focus of her life. Her anchor and her refuge.

She'd known she was in danger of losing it, but not so soon. *Mon Dieu,* not like this.

REQUEST YOUR FREE BOOKS!

2 FREE NOVELS
FROM THE SUSPENSE COLLECTION
PLUS 2 FREE GIFTS!

YES! Please send me 2 FREE novels from the Suspense Collection and my 2 FREE gifts (gifts are worth about $10). After receiving them, if I don't wish to receive any more books, I can return the shipping statement marked "cancel." If I don't cancel, I will receive 3 brand-new novels every month and be billed just $5.74 per book in the U.S. or $6.24 per book in Canada. That's a savings of at least $2.25 off the cover price. It's quite a bargain! Shipping and handling is just 50¢ per book.* I understand that accepting the 2 free books and gifts places me under no obligation to buy anything. I can always return a shipment and cancel at any time. Even if I never buy another book from the Reader Service, the two free books and gifts are mine to keep forever.

192 MDN EZQ7   392 MDL EZRK

Name _____ (PLEASE PRINT) _____

Address _____ Apt. # _____

City _____ State/Prov. _____ Zip/Postal Code _____

Signature (if under 18, a parent or guardian must sign)

Mail to **The Reader Service:**
IN U.S.A.: P.O. Box 1867, Buffalo, NY 14240-1867
IN CANADA: P.O. Box 609, Fort Erie, Ontario L2A 5X3

Not valid to current subscribers of the Suspense Collection
or the Romance/Suspense Collection.

Want to try two free books from another line?
Call 1-800-873-8635 or visit www.morefreebooks.com.

* Terms and prices subject to change without notice. Prices do not include applicable taxes. Sales tax applicable in N.Y. Canadian residents will be charged applicable provincial taxes and GST. Offer not valid in Quebec. This offer is limited to one order per household. All orders subject to approval. Credit or debit balances in a customer's account(s) may be offset by any other outstanding balance owed by or to the customer. Please allow 4 to 6 weeks for delivery. Offer available while quantities last.

Your Privacy: Harlequin is committed to protecting your privacy. Our Privacy Policy is available online at www.eHarlequin.com or upon request from the Reader Service. From time to time we make our lists of customers available to reputable third parties who may have a product or service of interest to you. If you would prefer we not share your name and address, please check here. ☐

MSUS09HM

REQUEST YOUR
FREE BOOKS!

2 FREE NOVELS
FROM THE ROMANCE COLLECTION
PLUS 2 FREE GIFTS!

YES! Please send me 2 FREE novels from the Romance Collection and my 2 FREE gifts (gifts are worth about $10). After receiving them, if I don't wish to receive any more books, I can return the shipping statement marked "cancel." If I don't cancel, I will receive 3 brand-new novels every month and be billed just $5.74 per book in the U.S. or $6.24 per book in Canada. That's a savings of at least $2.25 off the cover price. It's quite a bargain! Shipping and handling is just 50¢ per book.* I understand that accepting the 2 free books and gifts places me under no obligation to buy anything. I can always return a shipment and cancel at any time. Even if I never buy another book from the Reader Service, the two free books and gifts are mine to keep forever.

193 MDN EZQK   393 MDN EZQV

Name _____ (PLEASE PRINT) _____

Address _____ Apt. # _____

City _____ State/Prov. _____ Zip/Postal Code _____

Signature (if under 18, a parent or guardian must sign)

Mail to **The Reader Service:**
IN U.S.A.: P.O. Box 1867, Buffalo, NY 14240-1867
IN CANADA: P.O. Box 609, Fort Erie, Ontario L2A 5X3

Not valid to current subscribers of the Romance Collection
or the Romance/Suspense Collection.

Want to try two free books from another line?
Call 1-800-873-8635 or visit www.morefreebooks.com.

* Terms and prices subject to change without notice. Prices do not include applicable taxes. Sales tax applicable in N.Y. Canadian residents will be charged applicable provincial taxes and GST. Offer not valid in Quebec. This offer is limited to one order per household. All orders subject to approval. Credit or debit balances in a customer's account(s) may be offset by any other outstanding balance owed by or to the customer. Please allow 4 to 6 weeks for delivery. Offer available while quantities last.

Your Privacy: Harlequin is committed to protecting your privacy. Our Privacy Policy is available online at www.eHarlequin.com or upon request from the Reader Service. From time to time we make our lists of customers available to reputable third parties who may have a product or service of interest to you. If you would prefer we not share your name and address, please check here. ☐

MROM09HM

REQUEST YOUR FREE BOOKS!
2 FREE NOVELS PLUS 2 FREE GIFTS!

HARLEQUIN®

Super Romance®

Exciting, emotional, unexpected!

YES! Please send me 2 FREE Harlequin® Superromance® novels and my 2 FREE gifts (gifts are worth about $10). After receiving them, if I don't wish to receive any more books, I can return the shipping statement marked "cancel." If I don't cancel, I will receive 6 brand-new novels every month and be billed just $4.69 per book in the U.S. or $5.24 per book in Canada. That's a savings of close to 15% off the cover price! It's quite a bargain! Shipping and handling is just 50¢ per book*. I understand that accepting the 2 free books and gifts places me under no obligation to buy anything. I can always return a shipment and cancel at any time. Even if I never buy another book from Harlequin, the two free books and gifts are mine to keep forever.

135 HDN EZRV   336 HDN EZR7

Name _____ (PLEASE PRINT) _____

Address _____ Apt. # _____

City _____ State/Prov. _____ Zip/Postal Code _____

Signature (if under 18, a parent or guardian must sign)

Mail to the **Harlequin Reader Service:**
IN U.S.A.: P.O. Box 1867, Buffalo, NY 14240-1867
IN CANADA: P.O. Box 609, Fort Erie, Ontario L2A 5X3

Not valid to current subscribers of Harlequin Superromance books.

**Are you a current subscriber of Harlequin Superromance books and want to receive the larger-print edition?
Call 1-800-873-8635 today!**

* Terms and prices subject to change without notice. Prices do not include applicable taxes. Sales tax applicable in N.Y. Canadian residents will be charged applicable provincial taxes and GST. Offer not valid in Quebec. This offer is limited to one order per household. All orders subject to approval. Credit or debit balances in a customer's account(s) may be offset by any other outstanding balance owed by or to the customer. Please allow 4 to 6 weeks for delivery. Offer available while quantities last.

Your Privacy: Harlequin is committed to protecting your privacy. Our Privacy Policy is available online at www.eHarlequin.com or upon request from the Reader Service. From time to time we make our lists of customers available to reputable third parties who may have a product or service of interest to you. If you would prefer we not share your name and address, please check here. ☐

HSR09HM

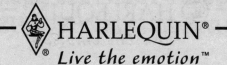

HARLEQUIN®
Live the emotion™

Love, Home & Happiness

HARLEQUIN® *Blaze*

Red-hot reads.

 Harlequin® Historical
Historical Romantic Adventure!

HARLEQUIN® *Romance*

From the Heart, For the Heart

HARLEQUIN®
INTRIGUE®
Breathtaking Romantic Suspense

Medical Romance™...
love is just a heartbeat away

HARLEQUIN®
Presents
Seduction and Passion Guaranteed!

HARLEQUIN® *Super Romance*®

Exciting, Emotional, Unexpected

www.eHarlequin.com

HDIR09R2

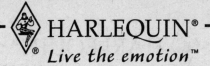

HARLEQUIN®
Live the emotion™

The series you love are now available in

LARGER PRINT!

The books are complete and unabridged—
printed in a larger type size to make it
easier on your eyes.

From the Heart, For the Heart

HARLEQUIN®
INTRIGUE
Breathtaking Romantic Suspense

HARLEQUIN®
Presents
Seduction and Passion Guaranteed!

HARLEQUIN®
Super Romance
Exciting, Emotional, Unexpected

Try LARGER PRINT today!
Visit: www.eHarlequin.com
Call: 1-800-873-8635

LPDIR09